This Cake Is for the Party

THE STORIES IN THIS BOOK HAVE APPEARED IN THE FOLLOWING PUBLICATIONS:

"Paul Farenbacher's Yard Sale"
The Walrus, March 2010

"Prognosis"
Event, Winter 2009

"One Thousand Wax Buddhas"
Prairie Fire Magazine, Summer 2008

"This Is How We Grow as Humans"
The New Quarterly, Winter 2007

"Throwing Cotton"
The Journey Prize Stories 18, 2006,
and *Prairie Fire*, Summer 2005

"Standing Up for Janey"
The New Quarterly, Winter 2005

THIS CAKE IS FOR THE PARTY

Sarah Selecky

THOMAS DUNNE BOOKS
ST. MARTIN'S GRIFFIN
NEW YORK

for ZZ

This is a work of fiction. All of the characters, organizations, and events portrayed in this novel are either products of the author's imagination or are used fictitiously.

THOMAS DUNNE BOOKS.
An imprint of St. Martin's Press.

www.thomasdunnebooks.com
www.stmartins.com

Library of Congress Cataloging-in-Publication Data

Selecky, Sarah Lucille, 1974–
This cake is for the party / Sarah Selecky. — 1st U.S. ed.
p. cm.
ISBN 978-1-250-01142-8 (trade paperback)
ISBN 978-1-250-01836-6 (e-book)
I. Title.
PR9199.4.S446T48 2012
813'.6—dc23

2012033335

First published in Canada by Thomas Allen Publishers, a division of Thomas Allen & Son Limited

First U.S. Edition: November 2012

P1

I am tremendously grateful to Zsuzsi Gartner for her unrelenting critical attention, support, and influence.

Thank you to Patrick Crean for his commitment and enthusiasm, to Janice Zawerbny for her diligence and care, and to Michel Vrána for his truly thoughtful design.

I am thankful for the fortitude of my literary accomplices: Julie Paul, Jessica Westhead, Heather Jessup, Erin Robinsong, Matthew Trafford, Laura Trunkey, Laure Baudot, Sarah Henstra, Scott Fotheringham, Mary Beth Deline, and Lesley Cowan. Thank you for your motivation, advice, and close reading. I owe a great deal to my teachers and classmates in the Optional-Residency Creative Writing MFA program at the University of British Columbia, especially Andrew Gray, Diane Fleming, Peter Levitt, Sioux Browning, and Susan Musgrave. Many thanks to all the women in the Salon in Toronto.

Thank you to Catherine Wright, Hilary Black, and Paulette Bourgeois, who allowed me to write in their quiet, beautiful spaces. Also to the Banff Wired Writing Program and the Humber School for Writers: these programs gave me the time and structure to write many problematic and necessary first drafts. Elisabeth Harvor read many of these stories in their early forms – thank you.

Thank you to Jason Dewinetz and Aaron Peck at Greenboathouse Books for the first *This Cake Is for the Party*.

To Tamara "Throwing Cotton to the Wind" Jakes, PD Bureau, and Usability Matters: thank you for patient, flexible employment while I wrote these stories.

A special thanks goes to my students, who continually inspire me with their practice.

Thank you to my mother, Mary Jane Selecky, for everything.

And a colossal cut of gratitude to Ryan Henderson for his legendary faith, encouragement, and love.

CONTENTS

All of you are perfect just as you are and
you could use a little improvement.

— SHUNRYU SUZUKI

Throwing Cotton

This past New Year's Eve, sitting on the loveseat in front of our little tabletop Christmas tree, I poured us both a glass of sparkling wine and told Sanderson: I think I'm ready to do it. 1

He kissed the top of my head and asked, Are you sure?

This is my last drink, I told him. I am officially preparing the womb.

Now it's the May long weekend. Sanderson and I have driven four hours north to Keewadin Lake, a cottage that we've rented every long weekend in May since we were at Trent together. We share it with our friends: Shona and Flip, who have been married even longer than we have, and Janine, who found the cottage for all of us almost ten years ago. I have a stack of first-year composition papers that still have to be marked, but I left them at home so this could be a real holiday. I have a strong feeling about this weekend. I think this might be the weekend we conceive. I'm trying not to get my hopes up, but my instincts are usually good.

We get to the cottage late, nine o'clock. It's already past dark and we're all very hungry. I can smell tension between Flip and Sanderson like something electric is burning. They both retreat to the living room. It's always been my job to sort the linens out when we arrive. But I feel particularly irritated that neither of our husbands has offered to help in the kitchen. These are progressive men. They know better than that. Shona and I move into the kitchen. Shona is an amazing cook, and she likes to do it.

Right in here, Shona says to me, even though I didn't ask her anything. She digs out a yellow packet of spaghetti from the bottom of one of the boxes. Told you! she says. She also finds a pot with a lid, a can opener, and cardboard tubes of salt and pepper left over from the last people who stayed here.

A knife, she says, distracted. Were we supposed to bring our own knives?

I remember the drawer from last year and show her.

I don't think they're very sharp, I say. We should have brought a good one.

This will work, Shona says, and selects one with a plastic handle and a pointy, upturned blade. It's not like we're carving a roast, she says. She starts slicing cloves of garlic on one of the speckled stoneware dishes. Each time the blade strikes the plate, the sharp sound makes me wince.

The sun was down by the time we got here. Now it's too dark to see anything. When I flick on the porch light, I disturb a fluster of moths. I cup my hands around my face and look out the window. There's a dock with a little motorboat tied to it and an apron-shaped beach. There is a pale glow that looks as if it's radiating from the sand.

The linen closet is where it always is, in the main hallway. I pull out musty-smelling sheets and threadbare pillowcases for both of the beds upstairs. For Janine's bed, on the main floor, I pick out the pink and orange flowered ones. Janine loves colour more than anyone I know. She's a graphic designer, but at Trent she studied English Lit like the rest of us. Not counting Sanderson, of course. She was actually enrolled in Sanderson's drawing class in her second year, but she withdrew when I told her I was sleeping with him. Those first years with Sanderson were more awkward than I like to remember. Our age difference was much more shocking when I was twenty-two years old. Now I'm teaching English at Ryerson and he's moved to the Art History department at York and I can't remember the last time I felt scandalous. I drop the flowered sheets off first, leave them folded on the edge of the mattress in her room.

She's not coming, Flip calls to me when he sees me there. Didn't she call you? I told her to call you.

She didn't call me. I hug my chest and follow his voice into the living room. I look back and forth between Flip and Sanderson. Janine didn't call, did she, Sand?

He shakes his head and fills his glass with more wine.

Did she say why?

She said she had a family thing.

I started dating Sanderson two semesters after I finished his class. I was the one who asked him out. We met in East City, across the river, at a small café not far from the Quaker Oats building. There was a woman wearing a red apron who served us coffee in thick white cups. I put two packets of sugar in my coffee and a long dollop of cream. He told me, You have a good eye. But you need to trust the line when you draw. He had silver strands of hair at his temples. I thought this made him look debonair and sophisticated. Now I think it's safe to say he's going grey.

I wish you wouldn't drink so much this weekend, I tell him.

We just got here, he says. It was a long drive.

Flip is stretched out on the chair, even though the chair itself doesn't recline. His body is slouched down so his seat reaches the edge of the cushion and his head is pressed into the back of the chair. His long legs are crossed at the ankles. It doesn't look comfortable. He takes up most of the living room.

I can tell you why she's not here, Sanderson says to me.

He rubs the side of his sandpaper face with one hand. He hasn't shaved for three days. He says the stubble makes him feel like he's having a more authentic cottage experience, so he cultivated it before we arrived. His beard is still dark—there's a patch of grey on his chin, but the rest of his face still grows a mix of dark reds and browns. Earlier this week, watching him sleep, I picked out the different colours sprouting. They grew like a pack of assorted wildflower seeds.

Janine feels threatened by your choice to have a child. She's withdrawing from you so she doesn't feel— He trails off.

Lonely and misguided, hopeless, bitter? Flip finishes for him.

Exactly, says Sanderson. She doesn't want to feel threatened.

Wait. *My* choice to have a child?

Flip ignores me. I can see now that he is stoned. But, but, he says. Janine must feel lonely and threatened already. Otherwise she'd be here, right? Whoa. I think that's a paradox.

Did she tell you that?

No, says Flip, looking at me again. I think it was her grandmother's birthday.

I glare at Sanderson. He looks pleased with himself.

The sound of the knife cutting on stoneware stops. I go back into the kitchen to open a bottle of seltzer. My choice to have a child. Okay. What I really want is a glass of red wine. Sanderson, of course, has the whole bottle next to his chair.

Shona hands me a glass from the cupboard above the sink. You want some lemon?

I want what you're having. I look at her glass of wine on the counter. But yes. Thank you. Lemon.

Shona is getting her master's degree at the Ontario Institute for Studies in Education at the University of Toronto. She has told me stories about the kids she's working with in her practicum. For instance: There is a boy who is obsessed with chickens. He calls himself the Chicken Man. Occasionally he clucks to himself when he is drawing at his desk. When he's excited, he calls out, Chick-*EN*!

Shona has this quality. She observes the world more carefully than I do. She is slow to make decisions or judgments. She will listen to you ramble, and when you are finished, you feel like she has just told you something important about yourself. She is going to be a remarkable teacher. I hope that my son or daughter will be able to study with her.

Shona slices a lemon in half and squeezes it over my glass. Have lots, she says, it's cleansing. She rinses her hand under the tap, blots it with a dishcloth. Cloudy tendrils of lemon juice work their way into the water. I can hear the fizz of small bubbles rising and breaking the surface.

I look up. Did you know Janine couldn't come this weekend? I ask her.

Flip told me. Birthday party? Something.

I think it's strange. That she didn't call me.

Shona doesn't answer. She reaches up and pulls her ponytail apart to tighten it and I catch a whiff of lacy, pungent garlic. Her oval face with all the hair pulled back is like an olive.

I say, Sanderson says Janine got her dog because I decided to have a baby.

She was looking into the breeders before that.

Yes, but. She didn't actually get Winnie until after I told her.

And Sanderson thinks this is important.

I look into my glass and focus on the bubbles that cling to the sides.

There's never the perfect time to have kids, I say. Right? You just have to jump right in. You never feel one hundred percent.

You make a convincing case for it, Shona says.

Janine's latest project is a font that she's made entirely out of pubic hairs.

I'm still working on it, she said on the phone the last time I spoke to her. Parentheses were easy. But I need an ampersand. I haven't even done upper case yet.

I could hear a reedy whine from Winnie in the background. Then she said, I was sitting on the toilet one day and I saw a question mark on the tile by my foot. The most perfect question mark.

In your pubic hair, I said.

It's important for me to keep the letters genuine. I don't want to mess around with the natural curls.

Right. That would be missing the whole point.

No! Off! Mama's on the phone right now! Janine said. Anyway. I think it looks good. Almost Gothic, but still organic.

I wish that I could be more like Janine. She doesn't even pretend to care about anything other than herself, and we all love her anyway. I shouldn't be so surprised that she didn't call me about this weekend.

Wait a minute, Shona says in the kitchen, raising her wine-glass and pointing at it with her other hand. Where's the rest of this? Is Sanderson hogging the wine?

In the living room, Flip and Sanderson have started to argue.

Sanderson leans forward in his chair in a half-lunge. His white sweatshirt has a logo with two crossed paddles on the chest, and a few spots of red wine that he won't notice until tomorrow morning.

Flip's face is tight. He says, If smokers came with their own private filtration systems, they could breathe what they exhale themselves. But we haven't invented that yet. So we stop smoking in bars.

Nobody's forcing you to breathe smoke.

Yes they are. In a bar, when there are smokers, it's everywhere.

Sanderson nods his head, leans back in the chair. Listen, he says. If I don't want to see a monster truck derby, I don't go to the arena. Get it?

You don't have to be an asshole.

You used to be a smoker too. I don't see where you get off.

Shona interrupts. Honey, leave it, you're stoned. Sanderson, pour me some wine.

Marijuana is different, Flip says.

They've been smoking in bars since the beginning of time, Sanderson mutters into his glass.

I don't like to see them fight like this. Sanderson thinks Flip needs to stop smoking dope—that it's making him dumb. Shona told me that Flip cringes when he reads Sanderson's emails because of the spelling errors. It's so important to each of them that the other appears intelligent. As though Sanderson's own intelligence is threatened when Flip appears dim-witted, or the other way around.

I get the bottle myself, since he's not making any move to do it. I pour some for Shona. Then I pour the remaining trickle into Flip's glass. Shona made dinner for us, I say, and turn to Sanderson. Say thank you.

Don't talk to me like I'm a child, he says. Then he flashes a wine-stained smile at her. Thank you, Shona.

There was a student in the fall semester. A young woman named Brianna. She's very bright, Sanderson told me. Her technique is rough, but inspired. Sanderson would call me in the afternoon, sometimes as late as five o'clock, to tell me that he was going to miss dinner. He never lied about where he was. He'd say they were going for drinks, grabbing a bite. He was helping her with her portfolio. One night he took her to Flip's bar. That's how self-assured he was. Flip told me that he saw them share a plate of calamari. That the woman fed him a ring from her fork. He said, The way she leaned across the table, Anne. I don't know.

I have always known this about Sanderson. He's one of those men who can keep his loving in separate compartments. He can love two women at once and not feel that he's betraying either of them. But when we got married, we promised that we'd tell each other about our attractions, that there wouldn't be any secret affairs. I can understand having a crush. It's lying about it that bothers me.

It's eleven o'clock when we sit down at the wobbly kitchen table to eat. The pasta should have been cooked for another five minutes. It sticks to my teeth like masking tape. But the four of us are so hungry we finish most of the noodles anyway, use up the whole pot of sauce to cover the piles on our plates. Flip mops up the last of it with a slice of garlic bread. Sanderson is quiet, possibly craving a cigarette. Shona is the only one who has wine left in her glass. I wrap my ankles and feet around the cold metal chair legs and silently will Sanderson to not open another bottle. It's cold in the cottage, even though the candles on the table make it look cozy. I could go put on some socks, but Sanderson already took my bag upstairs and I'm too lazy to go up there. My belly feels full and tight from too much pasta and bubbly water.

So, have you picked any good baby names? Flip asks me.

I heard someone in Calgary named her daughter Lexus, I answer.

I think it's exciting, Shona says. I'm living vicariously.

Flip looks at her. You want one too now?

This is how it happens, Sanderson says.

Shona looks at him. What exactly do you mean, she says.

We all want meaning in our lives. We all want to feel significant. Why else would we choose to have babies? It's our mortality thing.

Flip says, You have a mortality thing happening already?

Shut up, says Sanderson.

I try saying this out loud: I just think it's time. I feel ready. I don't want to wait until I'm old to have a baby. I want to be a cool mom.

Shona says, I hate to say this, sweetie, but I don't think a mom will ever seem cool to a teenager.

What do you think is old? Flip asks.

I just feel ready right now, I say.

Sanderson pushes his chair back from the table. He says, If I'm not ready now, I'll never be ready. It's time to throw cotton to the wind. He picks up his plate and brings it to the counter, plugs the drain, and turns on the hot water tap. Did we bring dish soap?

Shona points. Underneath.

Caution, I say.

What?

Everyone is quiet for a moment. Then a round, hollow, and breathy sound comes from Flip, who is trying to hide his laugh in his wineglass. It sounds like the fossilized call of a loon. Shona rolls her eyes at him.

It's throw caution to the wind, not cotton, I say.

You know what I mean. You don't have to make fun of me, he says.

No, it makes sense. You just throw cotton to the wind. It starts blowing around, right? Because of the wind? I start laughing, knowing that I should stop if I don't want to start another fight.

Sanderson ignores me. He looks in the cupboard under the sink and finds a bottle of green dishwashing detergent. He squirts some into the sink and there is a sweet apple smell. A white foam begins to grow on the water. Flip and I make ourselves stop laughing. We all sit at the table and watch Sanderson do the work.

You're going to quit smoking when the baby comes, right? Flip asks him.

Sanderson looks pained. Yes, Flip, of course I will.

Shona gathers the rest of the plates on the table and stacks them in front of her. She places the three forks on the top plate, which is covered with splotches of red sauce like a lurid Rorschach test. I think it would be nice, she says, for our babies to grow up together. She rests her hands on her belly.

Flip stares at her. I think we should wait, he says. Until you start teaching. You'll get maternity leave when you have a job. He touches his upper lip with his thumb. We could get a dog first.

Like Janine, says Sanderson.

Janine's dog is a baby replacement, Shona says. I want the real thing.

Flip holds the edge of the table with his hand. No, no. I'm way too irresponsible.

Shona sighs when she brings the stack of plates to the sink. You're just a scaredy-cat, she says. If I got pregnant, something would click for you. You'd get another job.

I say, What's wrong with working at a bar? Bartenders are respectable people.

You know what a baby means, says Flip. The money. There are those trust funds, those babies with the little graduation caps. No. Not until my own student loans are paid.

Shona laughs. Stop it, you're killing me. Paying off our student loans!

Sanderson turns off the tap and swishes the water with his hand. There's the bumping sound of plates swimming against stainless steel. Shona is beside him at the counter. She puts an arm around his waist and leans against him. He braces himself against the counter with one hand and holds her weight. Look at Sanderson, she says to Flip. He's not a scaredy-cat. I bet he still has student loans. Don't you, Sandy?

I glance down at my stomach, the way it makes a small ball of itself when I sit. It looks flat when I'm standing, but there's a little roll when I'm sitting down. I fix my posture in the chair. My belly changes when I straighten my back, but it still rests in a small lump on top of my legs. It's not a pregnant lump, it's just a weak abdomen, too much for dinner. But I try to imagine what it would feel like. When you're carrying a baby, you must feel like you're always carrying around a little Christmas present.

I'm actually all paid up, says Sanderson. But I had scholarships, so.

Flip stands up and fills my field of vision with his long legs, his green plaid torso. Sanderson is older than I am, he says. He's much more mature.

Don't you forget it, Sanderson says. Now excuse me, all of you, but I'm old, and I need a cigarette.

Don't turn on the porch light, I tell him. You'll attract the moths.

When he goes outside, I reach over the table for what's left of Shona's wine. Flip waggles his finger.

Oh, drink it, Shona tells me. It's not going to hurt anything. If Janine were here, you'd be drunk by now anyway.

14 This winter, when she bought a new condo downtown, Janine sent an email: I'm throwing a housewarming party. Just for us. Come at eight, stay till late. It was the coldest night in February, steam swirling on top of Lake Ontario because the air was so much colder than the water. When I blinked, my eyelashes stuck together, frozen. We arrived with housewarming gifts: a bottle of Tanqueray Ten, a jar of vermouth-soaked olives, a shiny silver martini shaker.

Janine opened the door and there was a gush of warm air in the hallway. The entranceway was a bright lacquer red. All along her wall, a line of tea lights glowing in glass saucers. She wore a short sequined cape on top of a black dress. It fell just above the elbows. A capelet. I felt the air melt around my body, my face defrosting. Janine had sparkles brushed along her cheekbones.

You brought cocktails! she said. She took the tall bottle out of my arms.

You look gorgeous, I said. I'll have a virgin cosmo.

Virgin my ass, she said.

Great paint job, I told her.

Like it? It's the same shade as Love That Red by Revlon. I had it specially blended and shipped from this place in Oregon.

It's hot, Sanderson said.

Inside, Flip and Shona were already drinking, sitting on chrome bar stools. Shona stirred pink juice in a glass with her finger. They were talking about the ways people learn. Shona had just come from class. She said, There are three ways that we all learn: we're either auditory, visual, or kinesthetic.

I'm visual. I know I'm visual, Janine said.

Shona said, We learn in all three ways, but we lean one way most of the time.

I went over it in my head: It's hot, Sanderson had said. He didn't say to her, You're hot. But that's what I heard. I had just come off the pill at that point. My hormones were still stabilizing.

I walked to the back window. There was a good view of the Gardiner Expressway. A string of red tail lights curved away from me, and the cars made small movements as they braked and accelerated. From this distance they looked like I imagined blood cells would look, moving through a capillary.

Flip came up behind me and said in my ear: Hello, I'm kinesthetic. What are you?

Sanderson was at the bar looking for a shot glass. Janine had filled the martini shaker with ice cubes. The bottom half of the shaker was already cold grey, frosting from the inside out. Her sequined cape, the martini shaker, the bar stools, Sanderson's hair: I turned around and saw everything in silver.

Janine said, You're visual too, Sandy. She flickered her fingers on his chest to illustrate her point. He wore a white T-shirt with a silk-screened drawing of a swing set on it.

I think I'm all three of them, I said. I can't just pick one.

Now Flip, he's auditory, Sanderson said.

And how would you know? Flip asked from across the room.

Because you talk so much.

Fuck you, said Flip.

Then, in a soft voice, Flip said to me, How are you doing.

I leaned into him. Ooh, I said. Is that velour?

Touch it, he said. I petted his sleeve like it was a puppy. His arm felt warm through the plush. I stopped at his wrist and held it with both of my hands.

Don't be mad at Sanderson, I said. He's just wired that way.

With the girls, you mean.

It's not serious with Brianna.

Well, good. As long as it's not serious.

I looked at him. We're human beings, I said. It's normal to flirt. We can't help being attracted.

Flip took his arm out of my hands. You don't have to explain it to me, he said.

I just love Weimaraners, I know, Janine was saying. She had brought a dog book out to the bar. She pressed the spine open with the palm of her hand. But my space is so small, she said. What do you guys think about this one? Is he too cute? Would you laugh at me if I got a terrier?

We'll always laugh at you, darling, said Shona.

What kind of terrier? Flip asked.

It's called a Cairn terrier. And it's oh-my-god cute. But then I would be one of those women, wouldn't I? Janine made a face. She held a fresh Tanqueray martini. The glass caught the light from the halogens overhead. It glimmered in her hand. There were three olives speared on a silver pick.

Shona said, Janine, you're already one of those women. Don't fight it.

If you see me with a Burberry dog coat, okay? You have permission to smack me.

Can you make me one of those, I asked Sanderson. With onions if she's got them.

On the fridge door, middle shelf, Janine said. She smiled at me. Virgin.

You want one too, Flip? Sanderson said. I'm pouring.

Flip looked at him. I'm kinesthetic, he said. Read my body language.

That night in the cottage I dream about a blizzard. Janine and her dog Winnie are trying to dig something out of a snowdrift. When I wake up, it's still dark out, and Sanderson has stolen all of the covers. I'm freezing. I lean over, grab the pile of comforters and blankets on the floor beside him, and pull them over the bed evenly again. He's wearing the blue boxers I gave him for his birthday last year. He sleeps on his side, one arm under the pillow, the other stretched out in a straight line away from me, his hand almost touching the night table. His hand is curled as though it could be holding something very small, like a pinch of salt.

I flatten myself against him, wrap my body around his lower half. I lift up my T-shirt and press my breasts into his skin. Tease my hand over the front of his boxers. The skin on Sanderson's neck is damp and bristly against my lips. I promise God, the Universe, the baby itself: Please let me have you. I will love you like nothing else has been loved before. Sanderson exhales a sour cloud of undigested wine.

There's a sound downstairs. Outside, on the deck: soft thumps, like falling potatoes. I stop the prayer and hold myself perfectly still. A rustling against the glass, a bump against the kitchen doors. It sounds like someone is trying to break in.

I whisper Sanderson's name, grip his hip and shake it so that his whole body rocks the mattress. He makes a noise like he's slurping something through his mouth.

I wrap a fleece blanket around my shoulders and shuffle across the hallway and peek into Flip and Shona's doorway. Flip is sleeping on his stomach, face pushed into the pillow, facing Shona. Shona is splayed on her side like a pressed flower, arms and legs draped over Flip's body in the effortlessness of sleep. Now that I am fully awake, I can hear the thumping sound for what it is: paws, jumping on the wood of the deck.

I go down the stairs slowly, starting on tiptoe and rolling to my heels so I won't scare them away. A family of raccoons. Three small ones rolling like bear cubs on top of one another. Close to the glass doors, a large raccoon—the mother, naturally I think it's the mother—sorts through the remains of the plastic Dominion bag that we used for garbage. The leftover spaghetti noodles seem to emit moonlight, making an elaborate pattern of loops and curls. I fold myself into the armchair and watch the little family make a huge mess. I look for letters in the patterns of noodles, try to spell out the letters in my name.

When Flip comes down, he sees me bent over in the chair with my face in my hands staring out the window.

Anne, he says. What's wrong? What's happening?

I look up at him. He has a T-shirt on, boxer shorts. His hair like a pile of twigs.

The raccoons got into our garbage.

He follows my gaze to the window. Shit, he says.

It's our own fault. We should have thought.

Flip rubs his head. You couldn't sleep either?

I just saw you. You were sound asleep.

I need a snack, he says, and goes into the kitchen.

The mother raccoon stops what she's doing for a moment and stands on her hind legs, her paws held in front of her. It looks like she's watching me. But I haven't turned any lights on. It's perfectly dark, we're concealed in here.

Flip comes out with a plastic honey bear and a spoon. Scootch over, he says, and sits next to me, half on the seat cushion, half on the arm of the chair. He squeezes the honey bear over the spoon. There is a shine in the dark when the honey flows out. He slips the spoon into his mouth and closes his eyes.

Flip.

Mm?

Do you know something.

What.

No, I mean, do you know something that I don't know.

Have some, he says.

He fills the spoon again and brings it to my lips. He doesn't let go, even as I work my tongue over the spoon, licking all of the sweetness off it. Then he slides it out of my mouth.

There, he says. Is that better?

His bare leg touching mine on the chair. It could happen so easily.

You can tell me, I say. Janine and Sanderson. Am I right?

Oh, Anne, Flip says.

I won't tell him you said anything. I figured it out on my own. I just want to know for sure.

There's nothing between Janine and Sanderson.

If there's nothing, then why isn't she here this weekend?

Anne. She wanted to be here. It really was a family thing.

I stop talking. Flip is resting the honey bear on his knee. He plays with the pointy cone on top of its head with his index finger. Circles it first one way and then the other. When his finger gets too sticky, he puts it in his mouth. Looking at me as he does this. I feel my nipples tighten into hard French knots under my T-shirt. He leans over and drapes his arm around my shoulder. His face is very close to my face. I can breathe him. He smells like toasted bread and Ivory soap.

I let my head fall back so he can kiss me. I notice differences: the softness of his lower lip, the way he cups the side of my face in his hand. That his face is smooth, even at this time of night. It is the first time in nine years that I have kissed anyone but Sanderson.

There, he says, and pulls away from me. That's what I know.

My eyes have adjusted to the dark, but they take shortcuts, turn shadows into shapes. It's too dark to see anything clearly. The shapes adjust when I think about what I'm looking at differently. When I stare at Flip's shoulder, the darkness clusters in front of my eyes and I can turn it into a perfect sphere. It crawls with darkness and I think about what Flip's shoulder should look like and then it morphs into a shoulder again. I remember an old drawing lesson, something Sanderson told me years ago. When you're drawing an object, you need to stick to one viewpoint. Set the object down and sit so you can see it without moving your head very much. You always want to have your head in the same place whenever you look at the object. A small movement can make a surprisingly big difference once you start drawing the details.

You should go to bed now, I say slowly.

Is that really what you want me to do?

Yes.

Fine, he says, and he pulls me off the chair and I go with him to the couch and we make love there. We move quietly and quickly. He says my name as he inhales. It sounds like and, and, and. When we're finished, we don't say anything. We lie on the couch together breathing honey. My arm is stuck in a crevice between the couch pillows. I feel something gritty rubbing against my elbow. Flip moves first. He slides his hands down along my hips and rests his head on my chest before he stands up. Then he goes upstairs and I can hear the water running for a minute.

I find my way into the kitchen and, without turning any lights on, I feel for a plastic bag in the drawer. I bring it outside onto the deck. The raccoons have pulled everything out and thrown it into piles. I crouch and scrape up the noodles with my hands. The wood looks stained even when the garbage is gone. I'm still in my bare feet. I know I should be cold, but I can't feel it.

Watching Atlas

I can hear it coming down Water Street, three blocks away. The siren yowls and moans and then dissolves into a stuttering Doppler. It's probably on the way to another quiet trauma—stroke, aneurysm, heart attack.

There have only been two memorable emergencies in the neighbourhood so far this summer. Last month there was a robbery at Sam's Milk Bread & Pop. Someone with a butterfly knife stabbed the cashier for Player's Lights and the acrylic box of pennies that went towards the spaying and neutering of stray cats. The *Examiner* said that the Peterborough Feral Cat Agency got their money back (four dollars and thirty-eight cents), but the cashier had to be hospitalized for the knife wound—a slit that ran deep under her clavicle, nearly puncturing her lung. Then, one week later, there was the woman who put enough Canadian Club into her bloodstream to mistake an iron guardrail for the horizon. She fell off her balcony and planted her skull in her own flower bed, crushing two vertebrae and a patch of pink and white impatiens. The woman was named Sylvia. Lise and I knew her. Well, we met her at a house party once. She'd been drunk that night too. Stuck in a string hammock in the backyard, laughing, fighting with her arms and legs, arching her back and straining to get out, like a moth in a cocoon.

Lise and I hear sirens all the time in Peterborough. But we interpret them differently. I like to think of myself as a rational guy, but when I hear a siren, I freak out slightly. I prepare for an emergency. My pulse beats like a strobe light in my throat. A siren sounds like a mechanical scream, which is even worse than a human one. But Lise says that she likes to hear the sirens, especially late at night when she's cozy in bed. She says it's like hearing a train in the distance. It calms her down. Reminds her that someone is out there, taking care of things, so she can sleep.

It's a Saturday, and I have the day off. The humidex reads ninety; the UV index is high. Peterborough doesn't have the toxic smog of a big city, but it's still hazy outside, so everyone calls it smog anyway. The humidity is so thick, it emits a low droning noise. Occasionally someone locks or unlocks a car door and a sharp bleating sound punctures our quiet subdivision. In the front yard of our rented bungalow, on a pink hibiscus-print beach towel thrown across a patch of brown grass, Lise paints her toenails half-and-half. The first side is silver. She uses a strip of masking tape to keep the lines clean between the colours on each nail.

I haven't seen Lise do the trick with the masking tape since last summer. She looks peaceful and studious. Krystal is supposed to drop her kid off here today again. Lise babysits for free because Krystal is an old friend. It's not a secret that I can't stand Krystal. She's a liar, is why.

"Why don't you tell Krystal you have a life?" I ask Lise.

"Because," she says, setting the word down carefully like a Scrabble tile. "I don't mind taking Atlas this afternoon."

She's talking to her toes. She's not even looking at me when she says it.

"I like being with Atlas," Lise reminds me. "And Krystal has a job interview."

"You mean she *says* she has a job interview."

"She sounded fine on the phone. She hasn't been drinking."

"Maybe not then. Maybe she wasn't drinking *yet*."

Lise doesn't respond to that. We've said all of this before. Perversely, I feel the need to clarify my argument. "You know you're just making it worse," I say. "You know that, right?"

Lise starts to bang the bottle of nail polish on her thigh so it clicks, the two silver balls stirring the lacquer.

"It's not like you've ever done anything to help," she mutters.

"She's your friend, not mine."

The balls go click-click-click.

"You know that's not the point."

"What is the point, Lise? Tell me."

Lise stares at her toes with the flags of white tape sticking to them and says, "The point is, you can be a real asshole sometimes."

"Oh," I say. "Oh, that's classic."

"I said you *can* be an asshole, not that you *are* an asshole."

As if to punctuate her statement, a siren screams down the hill from our house. We both pause as the scream descends, until it's completely out of range. I think: *Someone is dying*. Lise is probably thinking: *Oh good, they'll be safe now*.

"You should make that call," I tell her.

"What call? Call who? Call the police?"

"Well, that would be a start. That wouldn't be the worst thing."

"She'd freaking die. She'd hate me forever."

"I thought you said that wasn't the point."

Lise pulls the masking tape off her big toe. Her face is pink from the heat, and her forehead is shining with sweat. She has bits of grass stuck in her hair. She combs through her bangs with her fingers. Her shoulder blades move underneath the pink tank top and I notice that she's not wearing a bra, that it's just her skin underneath the top, her little breasts pushing the fabric out like soft rosy fists.

I say, gently, "What are you going to do with him today?"

Finally she looks at me. "I'm going to take him to the park," she says. "Maybe to the zoo."

"Yeah. Why not go for a walk?"

"What is that supposed to mean?"

"Nothing! You could walk to the park, that's all."

"Jesus," Lise says, and turns back to her toes.

"Now what? What did I say? What just happened?"

"You think I'm an idiot. The way you talk to me."

"I just said about the park, I didn't say anything."

"I'm smarter than you think I am. I can tell when you're making fun of me."

This is how it's been with us all summer. I imagine how good it would feel to throw her bottle of nail polish into the street, kick in the screen door, tear at the grass. But it's *so freaking hot.* I close my eyes and count to seven as I inhale. This helps. I close my eyes and let my head fall back. I always feel gummy and sick to my stomach when we fight.

"You know, Lise? This is my weekend. I don't want to do this on my weekend."

"It's my weekend too."

Except that it *isn't.* Every day I have to wake up at six in the morning and get a shirt ironed and drive across town to the bank where I work, and every day Lise *sleeps* until eleven and then makes a cup of coffee and brings it back to bed so she can *look for a job on her laptop.* I stand there with my hands in my pockets and listen to the sticky sound of the masking tape as Lise peels it off each toe. There's a crisp line between the polish and the bare nail.

"I saw him at the Wicket last week," I say.

"Who?"

"Atlas. Sitting at the bar."

"Krystal took him to the Wicket?"

"Krystal wasn't there."

Lise swivels on the towel so she is facing me. "Who was with him?" she asks.

"He was there on his own. At the bar with a plate of cherries and olives and a couple of plastic cocktail sticks. Swords, whatever."

Lise stares at me.

"Bruce was behind the bar," I add. "He must have given him the cherries and stuff to play with."

"What did you do?"

"I told Bruce, be good to this guy, he's a friend of mine."

Lise pushes her bangs out of her face. Her hair is sweaty and it stays where she pushed it. She looks cute, like a fancy canary. "You left him there?" she asks me.

"Everyone knows who he is. They wouldn't have let anything bad happen."

The Wicket is our local pub, but it's more like a community centre. It's a second home for guys like Bill Peters and Sid Rochon, who I don't think even finished high school. They *start* and *end* their days on those bar stools. But it's not a seedy place, either. Sure, the regulars are on their third pint by noon, and they have a stunning lack of ambition, but they aren't *criminals*.

"Don't you have to go to the gym?" Lise says. "You should just go."

The sound of an old motor curdles up the street. Krystal's blue Chevette pulls in front of the house. It's coated in a layer of dust, and the signal lights are chipped away from a variety of fender benders. Blisters of paint cluster on the hood like acne breakouts. The car chugs a little, settles after the ignition is turned off. Then the zipper sound of the parking brake.

Still sitting on her towel, Lise waves to the four-year-old in the car seat in the back. He stares out the window, takes in the cube of yellow bricks that is our house, the white and green striped awning over the front door, the dried-out lawn, all of which he knows as well as he knows his own house now. His eyes fix on me.

"Thank you, thank you," Krystal says out loud to nobody. It could be that she is talking to us. She steadies herself with one hand on the hood of the car as she works her way around it. The hood is too hot and she yanks her hand away when it touches the metal. She jabs her fingers under the back seat door handle and lets Atlas out.

"Come on, buddy, we're here." She's wearing a black skirt, black tights and a short-sleeved maroon shirt. Something glutinous wavers around her in the heat. She carries a depth of scent that is familiar, like beef gravy, but with a sharp edge.

"God, it's hot," she says. She teeters over the lawn wearing chunky heels. "These freaking shoes are not right," she says. "Winners, like three seasons ago."

"Why are you wearing tights?" Lise asks, looking up at her from the towel.

"They told me I can't do bare legs in this office. No open toes or whatever."

"Even in the summer?" I ask.

Both women look over at me. "Even in the summer," Krystal tells me.

"I have pantyhose," Lise says. "If you want. Summer hose, nude."

"Awesome," Krystal says. "What colour nude?"

They fall into this kind of shorthand whenever they're together. It makes it obvious that they've known each other since high school, if only because they start to act like they're in high school. The back of my neck gets itchy when I hear their banter. Atlas is standing on the grass in front of me.

"Hey Atlas!" I try. "Whatcha got there? Did you bring your truck? Huh?"

"Well, they're not orangey," says Lise. "They're light, you know, taupey."

Atlas nods at me, squats on the ground, and sucks on his bottom lip as he manipulates the opening of his yellow vinyl backpack. He pulls a red pickup truck out from the pack and hands it to me, I guess because I asked for it. "Thanks," I say, and I take it from him.

"Can I try them on?" Krystal asks Lise. "I'm dying in these stinkers."

It's been about fifteen minutes since Lise applied her first coat of polish. She tests her toenails to see if they're still tacky by gently tapping one of them with the back of a fingernail.

"Sure," she says. "I'll get them for you." She pushes herself up off the towel. An imprint of her lower half rests in the folds of the pink terry cloth. She walks barefoot across the dry lawn, flattening sharp points of yellow grass into a line of matted footprints. The screen door shuts behind her with a hiss.

"So," I say. Atlas is standing beside me and looking up at his red truck. I pass it from my left hand to my right hand and then back again. It's made out of plastic and it feels cheap. I remember playing with *real* trucks when I was a kid. Our stuff used to be made out of *metal*. "What kind of job is it for, this interview?" I ask. I try not to meet Krystal's eyes. She stands several feet away from me anyway.

"I'm registered at a temp agency," Krystal says. "So it's office work."

"Oh yeah? Where will you be working?"

"Well, I don't, like, have the whole job yet. I'm going to the interview."

Krystal directs her comments to my left arm. I have a tattoo of a jumping rabbit on my bicep. I know it's an *extraordinary* piece of art, but does it have to take the place of my *face* in a conversation? Atlas watches the truck in my hands like a hound eyeing a soup bone. It looks like he has one big eye and one small one. Or at least, one is wider than the other. Or maybe it's just slightly higher up on his face. I'm not making this up.

"But the interview," Krystal says, "it's at this law office, it's downtown."

"Ooh," I say, without meaning to say it like that. To cover up, I add, "That should be swanky. The office is open on Saturday and everything, eh?"

Krystal doesn't answer me. She crouches down to Atlas's eye level and calls him over to her. He hesitates, then gives up on his truck and walks over to his mother. Krystal tells him, "Be good for Lise, okay? I'll be back to get you in two hours. Do you want to stay outside with Greg or come in with me?"

"I want to stay outside!" Atlas yells.

Krystal smiles at me. "I'll just go take these tights off," she says. "You don't mind?"

Atlas has one hand busy in the crotch of his nylon track pants. He waggles his penis like a little tail under the fabric. "These are my favourite pants." he tells me.

I spin the wheels on the cheap toy truck. I press hard into the plastic with the palm of my hand, getting it to really spin. "Well, they're pretty snazzy," I say.

"My truck!" Atlas says. "Give it back."

I hand it over. "Did you eat lunch yet?"

Atlas shakes his head.

"You hungry then?"

Atlas nods. The boy has a large head for a four-year-old. It's disproportionate to the rest of his body—he still has a round belly and short, rubbery appendages that look baby soft and malleable. A colossal growth of shaggy, dusty blond hair does its best to cover the expanse of his forehead. When I consider the length and width of Atlas's cranium, I wonder if it's normal for a kid to have a head that big. Krystal leaves him alone too much, but would that result in a head-size problem?

"Let's go make ourselves a sandwich," I say to Atlas.

It's almost too hot to eat, but it's cooler inside. I lead the way into the house, holding the screen door open for Atlas with one arm. As he walks under, I flex my bicep to make it look like the rabbit is jumping over him. Atlas squeals, and comes back outside right away so he can do it again. He crouches down beside me and then jumps like he's the rabbit, and disappears into the dark house. There are no windows installed on the south side, which means that, a little after breakfast, we don't get any direct light indoors. I stand in the doorway for a few seconds, letting my eyes adjust.

We're in the kitchen eating peanut butter, mustard and lettuce sandwiches on whole wheat bread when Krystal and Lise emerge from the bedroom smelling like cigarette smoke and a high-pitched perfume.

"You're teaching him disgusting habits," Lise says, nodding to the squeeze bottle of mustard on the counter.

"*I'm* teaching him bad habits," I say.

Krystal looks at me. She's holding her black tights bunched in one hand, the feet and toes dangling. I screw the lid back on the jar of all-natural peanut butter and put it back in the fridge. "It's *whole wheat* bread," I say to the fridge door.

"Oh honey," Lise says, and for a second I think she's talking to me. Then she says, "Don't play with your food, okay?"

Atlas has taken his sandwich apart on the kitchen table. He's eating the mustard side first. The lettuce from the middle has fallen to the floor beside him, a smear of bright yellow on the tiles.

"Aren't you going to be late for your lawyer interview?" I ask Krystal.

"My watch was fast," she says. "I have an extra fifteen minutes."

Lise sees some mustard on Atlas's face. She folds a piece of paper towel, dampens it with tap water, and tries to wipe his cheek. Atlas turns his face back and forth, ducking the towel at each swipe. Something about his twitching head and his frustration makes me feel a flutter of understanding, shadowy wings in my frontal lobe: *I know just how he feels*.

"Wow," I say. "That was lucky. Good thing it wasn't fifteen minutes slow."

Krystal ignores me and says to Lise, "Thank you. I'm going to get going. I'll see you around three?"

Lise hugs her. "Those are my lucky pantyhose! If you know what I mean!"

When Krystal leaves, her hand lingers on the door handle for a second before she lets go of it. A rectangle of bleached sky and desiccated lawn disappears as the screen door hushes itself shut.

Inside our house, it is remarkably cool and dark. In the winter the lack of light is blatantly depressing, especially for Lise, who has a mild case of Seasonal Affective Disorder. But in the summer the cool linoleum and tiny square windows make it the only sensible place to stay during a heat wave.

I sit at the kitchen table and give Lise the eye. "Were you talking about me?"

Lise looks at me. "What do you mean?"

"In the bedroom."

"Don't even," she says.

Lise glances over at Atlas, who is huffing around in the living room. He's taking the couch apart, pulling off cushions and pillows and tossing them onto the rug. Lise goes to the fridge and pulls out a plastic litre bottle of diet Coke. With her free hand, she pinches two tall glasses by the rims, careful that she doesn't clink them together too hard, and then she comes over to the table. She pours one for each of us without asking.

"No thanks," I say.

"It's just Coke."

"It's toxic. I thought we weren't going to buy it."

"It reminds me of my childhood," Lise says. "It's sweet."

"It's going to rot our teeth."

"No it won't. It's diet."

"I'm trying," I tell her. "We say we want to eat better. Then you buy this stuff."

"I said it's *diet*."

Lise drinks it to make a point, looking at me over the edge of her glass. I can see her teeth swimming through the caramel liquid. She has such neat white teeth. They should be yellow from all the coffee and cola, but they look like polished oyster shells. Her lips are pursed over the rim to exaggerate the suction. Her eyes ignite as she chugs it down. She's going to start laughing. I turn my glass slowly on the table. It occurs to me to not say what I'm about to say, but the way she's drinking in my face makes my sinus cavities hurt. I can't stop myself.

"You know, at least *Krystal*—" I start.

Lise swallows the rest of her drink and lets out a rocking burp. "'Scuse *me*," she giggles. "At least Krystal what?"

"I was going to say that at least Krystal—who is a *drunk*, who is a *loser*, who is in *deep problematic trouble*—"

"Greg, shut up now," Lise warns.

"—at least *Krystal* is pretending to get a job."

A rhythmic, throaty, muffled sound comes from the living room. Atlas is screaming from inside a pile of pillows. Lise jumps up from the table to check on him. The screaming stops as soon as she steps into the room. See, that kid is *calculating*. He knows exactly how to get to her. I saw him scrape his knee on purpose once. He was rubbing his knee over the edge of the concrete step in front of our door, trying to make it bleed. When I caught him doing it, he actually started to cry and said, "Ow, I hurt my knee."

When Lise walks back into the kitchen, the look on her face is as expressive as a wall of aluminum siding. "He's pretending he's a tiger," she tells me. "He's made a fort with the cushions and he's playing a tiger that wants out of the cage." She takes a sip of her diet Coke and then says, "I'm going to forget that you called my best friend a loser. I'm just going to forget that."

I got my first car last summer after I landed the job at Scotiabank. It's a black Jetta—predictable, I know—but now I have deep feelings for it. It's probably not right to feel this kind of love for a vehicle. But it's more than just a car. It's my *zone*. Sometimes, when I'm driving along the outskirts of town on windy Highway 15, watching humps of trees like curvy hips and shoulders lying down in the distance and the line of the horizon straight in front of me, I'm able to completely exit my mind. I stop feeling or thinking anything at all. It's my own private enlightenment.

When I pull out of the driveway this time, I'm heading to GoodLife Fitness. I twist the air conditioner dial up to max. I slide in Bedouin Soundclash and turn up the volume. I turn it as far as it can go without distorting the bass. Then I just holler along. It feels like I'm ticking so close to the end of a countdown I might blow up. It feels good. At the corner of Lansdowne and the Parkway, I stop at the lights. There's a woman on a bicycle beside me wearing a tank top just like Lise wears. A small white dog sits in her front basket.

"Hey-hey, heeey!" I yell to the music. My windows are rolled up. I shout to make my voice go through the glass. *"Hey beautiful day! Hey beautiful day!"* I hit the steering

wheel with my hands over and over like I'm beating a conga drum. Who knows if she can hear me?

In the beginning there was a little bar on campus, a dark, inauthentic British pub called the Royal, an underground hovel, dim even on the brightest afternoons. There was a pool table in the back and twenty small tables covered with chipped forest green laminate, each set with its own cat- and dog-shaped salt and pepper shakers, a white ramekin full of sugar packs, and a plastic menu stand that held an oil-and-ketchup-stained list of what was on tap. It was April, the month of snowmelt, finals, and tree-planter recruitment. I had just finished my final commerce exam. I walked into the Royal and saw her right away—her hair was in a ponytail and there was a big peach-coloured rose attached to it, a silk flower—and it was like she was the answer to the bonus question.

She was sitting alone, talking to Matt behind the bar while he rolled cutlery into white napkins. I went to the bar and sat down and Matt slipped a coaster in front of me. I introduced myself to her. She told me her name was Lise, and that she'd just aced her French exam. We both ordered Coronas even though it was only eleven in the morning. She pushed her wedge of lime down into the bottle, put her thumb over the top, and turned the bottle upside down until the lime floated through the beer. When she turned it right-side up again, a blast of white foam sprayed all over the bar.

"Now, that's not supposed to happen!" she said, laughing. "That's not how it's supposed to go!"

I used wads of paper napkins for the spill and reached over her to wipe it up. Lise came close. She put her beer-damp hands on my arm and pushed up my sleeve to see the rabbit tattoo on my bicep. I have always regretted the tattoo. It was such a stupid idea. I was only nineteen when I picked it—it's a little kid's tattoo, a cartoon, it's meaningless. But Lise noticed it. It was the thing that brought us together. So I changed my mind about it. At that moment the rabbit was a karmic necessity, because when she held my arm in both of her hands, she looked up at me, smiling, and she said, *"Merci beaucoup, mon petit lapin."* Her voice was warm syrup and its effect on my inner organs was scandalizing. That was when I experienced the synthetic lining of joy—its perpetual companion—fear. Because now that I had found Lise, it had also become possible to lose her.

We moved in together and it was fast, in some ways, but it wasn't like we got *married* or anything. It's not like we're having babies. Everyone's having babies now. Half of my class got married the year after they graduated. Jake Middleton, Harv Saulter, Mitchell Lavois. I hardly see those guys anymore. They're involved in fatherhood, they're growing puffy because they can't metabolize their beer anymore, they're buying real estate. They have parties in the summer up at their family cottages in Muskoka. They hire caterers and babysitters and they drink to get drunk and talk stupid. I've been up there, and let me just say that those aren't even cottages, they're *houses*. Big houses. These guys went into commerce for a reason. Even though I know that they're all mostly unhappy, that they're all morphing steadily into versions of their own fathers and they hate it—if they could talk about it, they'd see that they actually do *hate* their lives—even though this may be true, even though I try to deny it, the thing is that *I want it too*.

Am I a big dick? What's the problem with a diet Coke once in a while? She can make her own choices, I am the driver of my own life, her decisions are not a reflection of my own, we are *autonomous individuals*, et cetera. I know I have these control-freak tendencies. I can't relax. I walk around the house like a clenched fist ready to pummel any flat surface that gets in the way. I should breathe more, I should find a vitamin for stress relief, what are those, are they B vitamins? Vitamin D? Lise is so calm all the time. I've seen her lying on the couch in her pink sweatpants, adorable, her little chin poking into her chest, and she's staring at the wall, totally serene. I want some of that. What is she thinking about, when she's lying there? I could ask her. Maybe that's what she wants—for me to show her my *vulnerable side*. Does she want me to tell her how I'm *feeling*?

This is how I'm feeling: I hate Scotiabank. I am twenty-three years old and I have to wear a *wrist guard* for my repetitive strain disorder, caused by *data entry*. Most of my friends from school have erased me from their lives within one year of graduation. The one friend who hasn't forgotten me—Jay—just moved to British Columbia to get his *MBA*. I'm paying too much rent for our house, which is so dark it could double as a torture dungeon, and I've started paying our rent with my Visa card because I'm having a slight *cash flow problem*. Lise is the only thing that's good in my life right now.

I change my mind about going to the gym. I just need to drive. I take the exit onto Highway 15 instead. Shift into third. Maybe I'm on the wrong track. Maybe this is all about the kid. Because today it was very clear: Atlas is a *major problem*. The kid's mother has problems, so the kid has problems, and now Lise and I have problems. Too many people in this town drinking instead of thinking. Like that woman Sylvia, perfect case in point. She was one of *Krystal's* friends, as if that's a big surprise. And look what happened to her. It's going to happen to Krystal too, if someone doesn't do something soon.

We could take Atlas away from her. There would be enough to make a case for it. But they *protect* her, her friends hide everything, they try to make it better for Atlas by keeping him there. They say, *No matter what, he needs his mother!* These women go to Krystal's place after she's gone on a bender and they clean up the catacomb. They scrape fossilized cat shit out of the carpet fibres and they gather up the empty yellow Gordon's bottles in cardboard boxes, dropping them off behind the Price Chopper Dumpster so nobody will see. They put boxes of cornflakes in the cupboard for Atlas, and put a bowl of apples on the counter as well as a Mason jar filled with the daisies that are growing in the driveway. They open Krystal's mail for her, they bring Atlas a pile of library books with Cellophane covers and full-page colour illustrations, and they brush Krystal's hair until she's sober again. What they do is, they make it look okay when Children's Aid comes to visit. They come for regular checkups now. Sure, CAS knows it's not right when they come, they know there's a cleaning brigade, but there's nothing they can do.

Highway 15 is first-rate this afternoon. Nobody on the road but me. The air conditioner fan refrigerates my wrists and forearms, and they ache from the cold. My brain is slowing down the way it does before shutting off. My thoughts are finally stalling. I adjust the direction of the vents on either side of the steering wheel to aim the cold air away and off my skin. I see Lise in her little tank top. I shift into fourth. There's Atlas with a splotch of mustard on his big wide face. A car is going slowly in front of me. I shift down instead of braking. It's a cop. I'm only a click over the limit. I drive behind the police car for a bit. I think about Krystal and her stubbly legs squeezed into Lise's pantyhose. The cop is really going slow, he's driving below the speed limit, which I figure means *Go ahead and pass me, I know my car is intimidating but I'm not going to pull you over*, so I pass him. But I keep glancing in the rear-view until I'm sure his lights won't start flashing.

When I come home from the drive—I ended up at the mall for retail therapy—Lise is making dinner and Atlas is sitting at the kitchen table twisting a lump of dough in his hands. There's a curl of blue cardboard on the kitchen counter, which means it's a Pillsbury night again. I bring in my shopping bags and set them on the table. I drop my keys in the dish by the front door that says *Florida's Ripe for Picking*.

"A few treats," I say.

Lise slices a green pepper on the cutting board. The cutting board should probably be soaked in bleach. There's a stain on the edge of it, something blackish. It's probably mould.

I open the bags and take out my presents: a *Finding Nemo* DVD for Atlas, a new Radiohead CD for myself, and a shell-pink matching bra and underwear set for Lise.

"I saw these at La Vie en Rose," I tell her. I lift the gold sticker, tearing the tissue paper slightly, so she can see them folded nicely inside.

The pizza dough is already unrolled onto a cookie sheet. It's pale white under a sweep of red sauce. It reminds me of naked skin, but not in a good way. Lise raises her fist and scatters the diced green pepper over it.

"They're nice," she says to me. I fold the pink cotton back up in the tissue paper.

“Atlas, do you like olives?” Lise peels the lid off a can of black olives as she asks.

“Nope,” Atlas says. Atlas rolls the piece of dough into a worm shape, presses it flat with the palm of his hand, then scrapes it up and rolls it again.

“I like olives,” I say.

“Can you make me a doggie?” Lise asks Atlas.

“I’m making a snake,” he answers.

“Krystal hasn’t called yet,” she tells me.

“You can put olives on half of it.”

“She’ll call soon.”

Lise has twisted her hair up on top of her head and held it in place with a rubber band. Her bangs have slipped out of the twist. They’re falling into her eyelashes. I reach over and push them out of her eyes, because her hands are covered in green pepper juice and she can’t do it herself.

“Must have been some kind of extra-long interview.”

“She’ll call,” Lise says, in a quiet voice.

“Maybe they hired her, and the boss told her to start tonight.”

She turns her back to me, drains the can of olives in the sink.

“Maybe her car broke down and she’s waiting for a new part.”

“Please leave it,” she tells me.

Anger makes my eardrums swell. I stand there and feel what adrenalin does to the inside of my head. My stomach goes oily. Why won’t Lise admit it? Krystal’s on another date with Jose Cuervo at the HoJo tonight, and they’re obviously having such a *scintillating* conversation that she simply forgot to come home! Why is Lise so loyal to Krystal, anyway? Because they have a *history* together? Because they've been through some *rough times* together? It seems to me that the rough times are *here and now*, and that one's heartwarming memories of high school bush parties and drinking games can turn out to be rancid nostalgia when one grows up and finds out that she *can't stop drinking*.

With one end stuck inside his nostril, Atlas chews on a ropy strand of raw dough, the whole piece hanging into his mouth like a piece of snot.

"Atlas, Greg got you a movie," Lise says. "Do you want to see *Finding Nemo*?"

"No," Atlas says, and flings the worm of dough at Lise. Half of the strand, the wet part that was in Atlas's mouth, sticks to her shoulder.

"Ew!" Lise flinches, her hands up, instinctively protecting her face. The dough pulls away and drops to the floor. "Atlas, please don't throw," she says.

I stare at the slimy snake of pizza dough curled on the tiles. It lies there like a bloated and misshapen valentine. Lise sprinkles a handful of black olive slices over the pizza and flicks the rubbery bits from her fingers to get them all off before she slides the tray into the oven. Atlas gets down on the kitchen floor in front of me. He presses a zigzag pattern into the circle of dough with the toe of his sneaker. I think about what this house will feel like when it's just me and Lise again.

"Call me when the pizza is ready," I say.

The light outside is settling into a deep Tuscan orange, and the house across the street has turned on the sprinkler. It sounds like a rattlesnake. I go into the bedroom and power up my laptop on Lise's side of the bed, in the one spot in the corner where we can pick up the neighbours' wireless. I find the website easily. The number is right there in large blue sans serif at the top of the page. *If you have a concern, please call 1-705-924-4646.*

I jot the number down on one of the old pages from the *Far Side* one-a-day cartoon calendar on the night table (when did we stop reading the cartoons? Because we haven't looked at them, not for a long time) and I flip open my cellphone and I dial the number. It rings twice before someone says hello. My stomach swings up to my throat as I start to speak. One day—probably not this summer, because I know it could take time to understand what I'm doing and what it means, it could be years from now—but maybe, if everyone is careful and lucky and if we pay attention, maybe we will all remember this day as though it was the beginning of everything instead of the end.

How Healthy Are You?

On Saturday morning, Carolyn gets Bruno to do the quiz. It's a multiple-choice questionnaire in *Business Weekly*, the free magazine that comes in the newspaper every Wednesday. The questionnaire asks a series of health-related questions and then you can graph yourself on a chart to see if you are in the high-risk quadrant.

Bruno is doing his online banking with his laptop at the kitchen table. Carolyn sits beside him on the bar stool, so she can see what he's doing. There are all of these emails—emails from work, emails from Rob with links to funny videos. He keeps opening the emails to avoid their Visa bill.

Do you have sore or stiff muscles? Carolyn asks.

Sure I do, Bruno says.

Mild, moderate or severe?

Bruno finally clicks on *Transfer Funds*. Mild, he says. No, moderate.

Carolyn looks at him. Really? she says.

No, mild.

One point, she tells him.

They've already eaten breakfast—croissants with butter and apricot jam. They ate everything quickly. Carolyn wants to have breakfast again. It's not that she's still hungry—she just wishes that she paid more attention when she ate the croissants the first time. If she were given a second chance, she would eat them more slowly. She can't even remember the way the flakes fell off when she tore the pastry apart, or if they fell off at all. And they used the same knife for the butter dish and the jar of jam. She regrets that.

We've spent five hundred dollars on pizza this month, Bruno says. He scribbles this number down with a stub of a pencil on the back of an envelope.

Bruno wears jeans and a grey T-shirt. His hair is soft and babyish on weekend mornings, before he puts in his moulding paste. He usually likes to wear it in short spikes. On Saturdays he lets it go. Seeing him with his hair down makes Carolyn think he looks slightly pissed off, like a cat with its ears flattened back.

I refuse to skimp on our food, Carolyn says. Do your eyes itch, burn or express discharge?

It's too much. Maybe we should stop ordering from Magic Gourmet, Bruno says. My eyes sometimes burn, from the computer.

One point. But they're antioxidant pizzas. Otherwise it would just be junk food.

But they're fifty dollars.

Only forty. They use spelt flour and flax oil and Himalayan salt crystals. All of the vegetables are locally grown at organic farms.

But with the taxes and the tip and everything.

The envelope still has his parents' Christmas card inside. Bruno and Carolyn have a ribbon for the cards—it's hanging over the fireplace, they clip the cards on with clothespins as they arrive—but this one hasn't made it up yet for some reason. Bruno pulls it out. *Joyeux Noël*, the card says inside, in red print. His mother has signed for his father as well as herself.

Are Rob and Linda going to be there tonight? Bruno asks.

I don't think so, Carolyn says. Rob works in government. They don't pay for things like this—they have the United Way. Do you have trouble sleeping? Trouble staying awake?

Are you keeping track of my score?

In my head, she says.

Both, he says.

Mild, moderate or severe?

It depends, Bruno says. Sometimes I get to sleep after I lie awake for a bit. But last night I woke up and couldn't get back to sleep. I was up most of the night.

I'm going to say moderate, Carolyn says. Four points.

Did you notice I was gone? Bruno asks.

Carolyn looks up at him. No, she says. You must have been really quiet. Thank you for not waking me.

Bruno slips the card back in the envelope. It was my pleasure, he says.

Carolyn has a funny feeling on her upper lip. It feels like it could be a cold sore. She doesn't get cold sores, but she's heard the feeling of one described as a little bug crawling under your skin. It feels like this now—a strange tingling sensation just under the skin.

Only a few more questions, Carolyn says.

Would you like more coffee? I could start another pot.

I think we should stop drinking coffee, she says. It's starting to disturb your sleep patterns, obviously.

Bruno nods at the computer screen.

And I think it might be giving me cold sores, Carolyn says.

You don't get cold sores, Bruno says. Stop worrying about coffee.

Carolyn concentrates on her upper lip to see if she can still feel the tingle. She closes her eyes and she just focuses on that part of the skin. There it is. It's got to be something.

I don't know how you do it, she says to Bruno. You just go through life completely unaware. You don't think about anything.

Bruno clicks on a link from one of his emails and a video opens in a new screen. It's a hidden camera in a hotel room. The video shows a housekeeper spraying the drinking glasses with blue liquid that comes in a bottle labelled *Do Not Drink*. She's wearing rubber gloves. Then she rinses them off under the tap and puts them next to the sink. The housekeeper lifts an old washcloth to her nose, sniffs it, and uses it to wipe the glasses dry.

That's disgusting, Carolyn says.

I'm sorry you had to see that, says Bruno.

We are never staying in a hotel again, says Carolyn.

Bruno bought the tickets for the library fundraiser from the communications director at his office. Everyone sits around a big table and gets to meet and chat with a real Canadian author. The money raised goes to the Toronto Public Library. The tablecloths are emerald green, and they drape down to the floor. The bright red napkins are folded in a fleur-de-lys pattern and stuffed into wine-glasses. It's the middle of December, and the third floor of the Royal York—Convention Hall, Level C—is full of people.

The author at their table is tall and attractive, with olive skin and salt-and-pepper hair combed in a sleek wave over his forehead, so shiny it could have been set with shoe polish. The style looks intentionally outdated. He wears a rented tuxedo. Carolyn sees a rib of elastic around his neck where the bow tie connects. The sleeves are a little short on his wrists and the cufflinks are small black plastic plugs, the kind that come with a rental. Carolyn feels sorry for the author, all alone at this table full of computer programmers. Nobody here has heard of his book. It's called *The Slipped Knot*, a multi-generational historical novel, and on the cover is a photograph of a Victorian woman with a strong nose and a high collar. Her thoughtful gaze points to the spine of the book. There is nothing to say about it.

The centrepiece, a large glass tube full of curly willow branches and fuchsia orchids the colour of an infected throat, towers above the table. It's the height of a six-year-old. Carolyn is happy for the camouflage. She elbows Bruno.

Look, she says. Does the emcee look familiar to you?

Kind of, says Bruno. Did he play volleyball for Carleton?

I thought familiar as in a television show, says Carolyn.

Oh, says Bruno. Then no. Not to me.

The table next to theirs is sponsored by St. Michael's Hospital. They have a recognizable author: it is the young woman who wrote *Everything Can Be Bright*, a postmodern fictional memoir about growing up adopted in Montreal and discovering at age fifteen that her biological mother is actually Celine Dion. It's been optioned for a film. She's wearing a grey felt hat with a peacock feather fastened to the front of it. A swarm of servers dressed in black and white come out of nowhere. They circle the table all at once and deposit plates in front of each guest.

The fish looks weird, says Bruno. Doesn't it look—orange?

It's tandoori, Carolyn says.

It's supposed to be mysterious, the author at their table is saying. Because what I'm doing is, I'm playing with the form of historical fiction.

What's that, then? asks Bruno. A server holds a plate with a dark brown puck teetering on top of a pillar of green and orange bands. He sets it down in front of the woman with the feather hat. As she receives it, she clasps her hands and makes her eyes go wide.

It's a vegetable tower, says Carolyn.

Ah, says Bruno.

Well, the author says to a woman sitting next to him, you're right about that. But let's not talk about marketing before we eat, shall we? It can cause indigestion.

The women on either side of the author laugh, shaking their heads. Their husbands—Brian and Dan, Carolyn knows both of them from Bruno's department—smile and fondle their copies of the author's book. They flip through the pages as though thinking if only they saw enough of the words inside his book, they would be able to think of a clever question.

Carolyn sees that Bruno's pant cuff is caught in the top edge of his sock—it must have lodged itself there getting out of the cab—so she bends down to pull it out and straighten it.

Thanks, says Bruno.

Carolyn? a woman's voice asks. Carolyn looks up. The left shoulder strap of her cocktail dress slips off her shoulder, revealing the top of her bra. She quickly pulls it back up again. She should have worn her strapless.

She looks up and sees Larissa Levinson, dressed in electric blue chiffon.

It *is* you! Larissa squeals.

Oh my God, says Carolyn.

I'm right over there, Larissa says, pointing to the table sponsored by the Royal Bank. I just saw you and I had to come over right away!

Bruno, says Carolyn, this is Larissa Levinson. We knew each other in Ottawa.

We worked together, says Larissa. Carolyn was such a great part of our team. Are you still taking pictures? Her eyelashes work themselves up and down hydraulically.

Oh, says Carolyn. Not really. I mean, not professionally.

Our author didn't show up! Larissa says. Can you believe it? Who's going to read his book now?

Across the table, the author in the ill-fitting tuxedo perks up when he hears this. He pauses in his conversation with the women beside him and turns his head in the direction of Larissa's table.

Bummer, says Bruno. I guess you can't really ask for your money back.

Larissa rolls her eyes. It *is* a charity ball, she says. But I knew I was invited for a reason. It was so I could find you! Carolyn, you look great. Now, I want to know everything about everything. How are you?

When an opossum feels threatened, it will go limp, rotate its eyes back in its head, and look as close to decomposed as it possibly can in order to avoid attack. Carolyn has seen this only once. Coming home on a summer evening, she saw what she thought was a white cat lying in a sewer grate in front of their house. When she bent down to look at it, she saw the opossum's bald, dead-looking face.

I'm living in New York, Larissa continues. I'm just here for a couple of weeks. I didn't know you were living here! This is crazy, finding you!

Carolyn's upper lip starts to tingle again. Well, it's for a good cause, she says.

What do you do in New York? asks Bruno.

Larissa holds her wineglass with both hands. When she drinks, she looks like a child with a sippy cup. I'm involved in marketing, she says.

I'm in marketing myself, says Bruno. What company do you work for?

Oh, I'm freelance, she says. She smiles at Carolyn.

Carolyn flushes, jungle-hot. I'm a teacher, Carolyn says.

Larissa goes back to her table once the speeches and presentations begin. Her blue dress has a short train that puckers on the carpet as she walks. Bruno and Carolyn are the only two people at their table who ordered the fish. The author has a vegetarian meal. All of Bruno's work colleagues (and their spouses) ordered the filet mignon. Carolyn watches the author through the orchid vase. He goes to his plate hungrily, slicing his vegetable tower into quarters and eating the entire thing in four bites. He reaches for his glass, but there is no more wine. He tries to catch a server's attention by putting up his hand, like he has a question.

Why are we here? Carolyn asks Bruno quietly. How much did we pay for this?

Bruno slides his fork under a wedge of roasted potato and attempts to bring it to his mouth. What's the story with Larissa? he asks.

His potato falls off his fork and back onto his plate. Carolyn resists the urge to take his fork in her own hand. *Stab it*, she thinks. *Stab the potato.*

There is no story with Larissa, she says. Was it over a hundred dollars each?

Bruno slices the potato in half with the side of his fork and then slides the tines under it. Guess again, he says. So where did you work in Ottawa?

We didn't work together, Carolyn tells him. I haven't seen her in ten years. God, fifteen years.

So what was she talking about? Bruno slips the potato piece into his mouth and looks at her, chewing.

Carolyn moves her food around her plate. The salmon looks unhealthy. There's no natural spice that colour—the tandoori paste is probably loaded with artificial dyes. She remembers that Bruno's quiz score—thirty-nine—was uncomfortably close to the red zone.

Bruno, she asks, why couldn't you go back to sleep last night?

You're changing the subject, Bruno says.

No, I want to know what kept you awake.

I don't know, he shrugs. I just couldn't sleep. I thought about work. I kept thinking about Grand & Toy's ugly new logo.

But why wouldn't you wake me up? she asks. You could have tried—*you know*.

Bruno looks at her.

I would have been into it, she says. I would love it if you woke me up like that.

Bruno exhales. I'm sorry, Caro. I thought you would rather sleep. You looked so peaceful. I didn't want to bother you.

Carolyn stabs one of her own potatoes. So now you think it's a bother, she says.

Excuse me, says the author, who is finally able to wave down a server. We need more wine here, please.

The last time Carolyn saw Larissa, they were in an industrial park in Nepean, Ontario, with ten other test subjects. The NuPres headquarters were located in a short concrete slab of a building that was ribbed with black tinted windows, making it resemble an awkward sedan. Two coffin-sized concrete planters embedded with pink and grey pebbles sat on either side of the front doors. They were stuffed with green and purple ornamental cabbage plants. A freshly painted picnic table sat hopefully on the lawn adjacent to the parking lot.

Carolyn and Larissa and the others had all signed a waiver, of course, before submitting to the tests—three pages of dense legal jargon that had made no sense to any of them—understanding that they were signing away their right to complain if something went wrong. Also, they were promising not to tell anyone what they were doing.

After the orientation meeting, the test subjects were shown to the common room and left alone. There were refreshments: a bar fridge stocked with bottled fruit drinks and cans of no-name soda. Larissa pointed out that the testing was simply unethical rather than illegal.

There are organizations that might not approve of what NuPres is doing, she said. But they're not the police. Nobody's going to come after NuPres for this, she added.

Unless something happens, said Pike. He wore blue and white striped overalls and a yellow T-shirt. He had just graduated from high school. He wanted to be an actor.

If something happens? said Carolyn.

Um, what's in these painkillers that makes them so *experimental*? asked Pike.

Carolyn had called the number on the NuPres ad because she needed the money. She'd lost her job when the owner of the bakery went bankrupt; she'd shown up for work one day and there was a sign on the door saying the place had been repossessed. Her rent was due the following week, and her student loan hadn't arrived. The advertisement on the back page of the weekly paper was tiny, but the figure stood out: $1,400.00. For one week of work.

The work involved swallowing a yellow capsule three times a day for seven days, sleeping on a cot in a small private room with no window, making conversation with eleven other test subjects, and allowing herself to be videotaped as she went about her limited activities during the day. When she called NuPres to register for the study, they asked her about her favourite food. She told them it was sushi. This is what they fed her for dinner for seven days straight.

Larissa had also requested sushi—maybe it was this taste in common that had cemented their friendship. Pike had asked for Thai food. But the other people had straightforward tastes. The room was consistently overpowered by the ropy smell of pepperoni pizza.

On the first day, they were given their capsules with breakfast. The numbers 009 were printed in black on the outside of the capsule. Carolyn swallowed hers with orange juice. She showered and dressed. She'd brought *One Hundred Years of Solitude* to read, a journal, her Spanish textbook and some Post-it Notes for vocabulary, and her Canon SLR.

On the second day, just after lunch, four of the other subjects began crying wordlessly. Pike and Larissa were sitting on Carolyn's bed and she sat on the floor, her back against the dresser. The three of them listened to the sobbing in the room beside them.

I guess they're homesick, said Larissa.

Has Dr. Brown talked to them? Carolyn asked.

No, said Pike. Nobody's come around all day.

I feel a little sad, to be honest, said Larissa.

Me too, said Pike.

Carolyn had a stiff feeling in her stomach, like she'd eaten too much white rice. I'm just constipated, she said.

Carolyn! Pike said. Too much information!

After dinner that night, Pike and Larissa both dumped their plastic takeout boxes into the green trash can in the hallway and went to their rooms without even saying good night. Carolyn stayed in the common room to watch television. An advertisement for a cellphone company appeared: a woman surprised by a phone call from her faraway lover. *Oh my love*, the woman said. The music swelled, fat violins rising. Carolyn's eyes heated up and stung. She was surprised to feel the tears trip over her cheeks. Something crawled up through her stomach and over her heart, deep blue and miserable.

The next morning Carolyn received a small cup of prune juice with her breakfast tray. Everything else—the box of Cheerios, the banana, the plastic orange spoon—was the way it had been every other day.

Larissa confessed to Carolyn and Pike that afternoon. She'd been a test subject before. Two times before this, she admitted. And you know what? she said. All of them had been for painkillers too.

Sure they have, said Pike.

We can't be so paranoid, said Carolyn. They're just painkillers.

Oh, I don't care what pills I pop, said Pike. If I cared, would I be here?

On the afternoon of the fourth day, a raw and unbound sense of agitation shot out of Carolyn's appendages with the force of magma. She pointed her lens at the dusty ficus tree that was faltering in the flimsy light of the common room and couldn't get her hands to work. Her fingers, nothing but stumpy carrots, were hot with blood. She heard it in her ears, the rushing sound of pumping and beating. A door slammed in the hallway.

You know what your problem is? one of the subjects shouted down the hall. You take everything I say negatively! You make it into a problem!

A door opened. That's not what I said! someone yelled back. Then the door slammed again.

That night, Pike asked the girls, Have you felt more emotional than usual?

Well, I expect so, said Larissa. Her hair had so much static, fine strands on the back of her head raised themselves up against the wall behind her. We're basically being kept prisoners here, she said. Of course we're emotional.

I have been feeling strange, said Carolyn.

Oh no, please don't share! said Pike. We've heard about your strange feelings!

I need some fresh air, said Carolyn. Why can't we take a walk?

Hello? said Pike, staring at the ceiling. He twisted around so he faced each corner and every wall as he called out. We'd like to take a walk! Please!

On the fifth day, Larissa said that Pike had come to her room early in the morning, wearing only his white boxer shorts. He told her that he'd been thinking about her since the first day, and that time was running out. He had to tell her how he felt. Larissa said that she'd felt the same way.

He's only nineteen years old, Carolyn said.

That's only five years, Larissa said. When I'm thirty-five, he'll be thirty!

Carolyn thought of Pike's wide lips and the way his hands held his chopsticks as he ate his green curry. Strong, but delicate. Hmm, she said.

You know, said Larissa, I caught Mark S. watching your ass this morning.

Which one is Mark S.? Carolyn asked.

He's the tall one in 8A. With the five o'clock shadow.

Carolyn felt it then. Her body responded with an even heat, like a convection oven, and this peppery warmth seeped into her appendages. Her lips fattened. Her scalp prickled.

That night, Mark S. showed up at her door dressed only in his towel. He was so tall, his head grazed the light fixture that hung from the hall ceiling. He brought two bottles of grape drink and two bendable straws. Carolyn reached up to take the bottle he offered her.

Thank you, she said politely. His naked chest was the size of a warehouse, but it was smooth and delicately glazed with sweat. He used his free hand to adjust the fold of his towel. The shape of his fingernails reminded her of butterscotch candies.

Do you feel it? asked Mark S.

A deep pulse slithered down Carolyn's throat and detonated in her stomach. I feel it, said Carolyn.

She let him inside her room. Mark S. lifted the single mattress off the bed frame and placed it on the floor. As he bent down to smooth the duvet below, Carolyn saw, with a specific and inexplicable flash of intuition, what they were going to do to each other next. She saw her naked hips in his large hands. Mark S. stripped Carolyn's clothing from her body slowly, and he draped each piece onto the bed frame. In his fingers, her pink blouse looked like a creased strip of sushi ginger. He placed his palms on her hips, just as she'd envisioned. Her sexual premonitions escalated as they moved together, and the montage in her head made her nerve endings thick and hot. She slid into the collapse between present and future. Her skin cells widened to absorb more from his touch. She felt Mark S. in her thymus and her eardrums, in the arches of her feet and through her spinal fluid. When he left her room, only a few hours before breakfast would be served, she tried to say good night to him, but her words were only compressed air.

On Friday evening, six days into the study, while the group was watching an episode of *The X Files*, Larissa told them that she thought her heart was beating too fast. What she'd actually said: *My heart is beating super fast.* The NuPres doctors would have heard her say it, of course. But they didn't come until it was too late. When Larissa collapsed, her head hit the arm of the sofa and knocked the remote control onto the floor. The plastic panel broke off and two AA batteries rolled out in opposite directions. Dr. Brown had two interns carry Larissa out of the room, and that was the last anyone heard of her. The next day, the final day of the study, Carolyn and the others walked up to the television to turn it on and off manually; nobody bothered to look for those lost batteries.

None of the other test subjects experienced any severe heart palpitations.

They confiscated Carolyn's film at the end of the week and developed it in the NuPres lab, but they wouldn't let her see the pictures. Dr. Brown told her that it was a breach of privacy for the project, as well as for the other test subjects. That if she'd read her waiver carefully, it would have been clear: no media was allowed to know about the project.

But why did you wait until this morning to take it away from me? Carolyn asked. You must have known I was shooting film all week.

Dr. Brown wore large glasses with bright red frames that were out of fashion. The white lab coat was also too big for her. She rolled her cuffs several times to keep the sleeves from flopping over her hands. I'm sorry, she said. But we wanted to see how you would react to the stimuli. As a photographer.

I think I took a few good ones, said Carolyn.

They're out of focus, said Dr. Brown.

Carolyn received her cheque on Saturday afternoon and took the public transit back to her apartment. She deposited the cheque, paid her landlord, found a job at the campus bookstore, and finished her degree. Some of her landscape shots were published alongside an article about RRSP contributions in a local magazine, which made her think of pursuing a career in photojournalism. Eventually, after a few months of unpaid work and rejection letters, Carolyn applied for a year of teacher's college instead. She accepted a job in Toronto teaching grade ones. She joined a volleyball team and played on Wednesday evenings, to keep active. This is where she met Bruno.

Every so often, Carolyn tried to find NuPres on the Internet. She was unsuccessful. She found out that Pike was living in Vancouver, running a queer-positive film production company. Mark S.—the S was for Stratton—owned and operated a fishing lodge in northern Ontario. But Larissa Levinson seemed to have disappeared.

A slice of warm chocolate cake with a wet, slick pudding centre is served in a wide dish dusted with icing sugar. A sliver of a strawberry and two blueberries roll beside it. Their dessert forks are small and highly polished. When it is set in front of him, Bruno eyes the chocolate with longing. The candlelight makes his eyes look shiny and liquefied, and Carolyn wonders briefly if the cake has made him cry. Then Bruno pinches a blueberry from the side of the dish with his fingers and puts it in his mouth. He closes his eyes and chews at length, appreciating it.

There will never be a night exactly like this ever again, she thinks. One blueberry is already gone. There are only three blueberries left between them.

The author with the silver hair has had several glasses of wine by now—his lips are stained from the Merlot. One greased curl has fallen out of place and hangs in front of his eyes. His movements are large and sloppy. He raises his dessert fork in the air before approaching his dessert.

Cocoa can cause sleeplessness, anxiety and an increased risk of prostate cancer, he says. He slides his fork into the side of his cake and releases a thick flow of dark chocolate. He turns to the woman sitting next to him. But the same chemical acts as a sexual stimulant, he tells her.

The night is nearly over. There is just the dancing left.

Six men in tuxedos come onto the stage and fasten themselves to their instruments. They fiddle with the dials and adjust their straps like pilots preparing for takeoff. The drummer uses a brush to make his snare drum hiss, and a large woman dressed in black velvet parts the silver curtain behind them. She walks to the microphone and closes her eyes, ignoring everyone. The woman with the peacock feather moves her chair so she can see the band, then turns back and says something to one of the guests at her table. Carolyn tries to read her lips. It looked like she said, *I know I am.*

The author at their table says loudly to someone, No, he did want to do something about it, but he was two hundred years too late.

Then the guitars strike and punch, the drums crack, the woman in velvet shouts, *What it is what it is!* and the music charges through Carolyn's spine. The other guests watch from their tables, too flattened by the volume to get up to dance. A few people nod their heads as though they agree with the woman onstage. Carolyn can see Larissa's blue dress across the room.

Bruno dips his fork into the hot pudding and licks it off. His left foot bounces to the bass. There is a salt stain on the cuff of his pant leg that resembles New York State.

Come on, Bru, Carolyn says. She holds his wrist. I want to dance with you.

Bruno has a line of chocolate at the corner of his mouth, set in place by the fork just a second ago. Carolyn reaches out to his face and touches the line with her thumb.

The author is shouting now. His voice is wide, and he skids over the words like they are large rocks in his mouth. He yells, But in the end! In the end, whatever he may think about her in the moment, he also knows what's going to happen to her in the end!

Bruno says, You should try this chocolate thing.

No, Carolyn tells Bruno. We have to dance right now.

Go-Manchura

Dear Friends,
My work at the clinic has introduced me
to a number of incredible nutrition products
that I would love to share with all of you!
Please join me
in the Haliburton Highlands
on Friday, October 5th
for a special retreat weekend!
Map and directions enclosed. Please RSVP.

The invitations went out two weeks ago. I used the laser printer at work—the Verde Salon & Spa—slotted ten pages of tree-free paper into the machine before pressing Start. The specialty paper was the same weight as copy paper but pale blue, flecked with parchment-coloured bits of garlic. Made entirely out of garlic, it was odourless, thank goodness. I bought it at the environmental store on Bloor Street, and it cost me seventy-five cents for each sheet. Of all the paper in the store, this one appealed to me because it felt so crisp.

I sent the invitation to ten people. The literature in the company's sales portfolio kit told me to expect a fifty-percent turnout to the first invitation. The growth will happen through word of mouth, it read, and you have to have patience for this community to build. Only four of my friends could make it for the weekend—two couples. This was perfect. It was a less intimidating number, and it meant that I could start my project slowly.

The company is called Go-Manchura. It produces a line of packaged foods, drinks and nutritional supplements that contain a powerful ingredient known to prevent cancer (especially of the inner organs), diabetes, hypertension, insomnia and indigestion. It's also been successful in the treatment of arthritis, anxiety and herpes. I don't know about arthritis or herpes—touch wood—but I'm certainly familiar with anxiety and insomnia. Go-Manchura's products have changed my life. I mean that sincerely.

Since I've integrated these products into my regular diet, I've felt a major shift in my overall energy levels. My sleeping patterns are more balanced—I now wake up refreshed each morning and fall asleep easily each evening—and this has made a noticeable difference to my moodiness. I view the world in a positive way, now. And this new energy has started an avalanche of abundance in so many other parts of my life!

My sweet, retired parents gave me one week at their time-share cottage for my event. I took a few days off from the clinic and drove up on Wednesday. The clinic didn't mind: Verde Spa has only two rooms, and a variety of therapists to fill them. They temporarily replaced my aromatherapy facials and rented the room to a graduate from the downtown shiatsu school. His name is Bobby, and before learning shiatsu he practised massage in the Dominican Republic for fourteen years. Every time he sees me, he says in his hot, lacquered accent: *Chew got to relaaax, Lee-lee-an.*

Tension winds around my head and shoulders like a spool of wire. This is from living in the city, period. There is nothing that I can do about it. So I tried to unwind as soon as I arrived in Haliburton. A brisk jog down and back up the hill and through the birch trees, a lunch of tomato soup and whole wheat toast, a solo paddle around the small lake, yoga in front of the fire, a pasta dinner and a few glasses of wine.

On Thursday, I realized that scheduling my day like this was exactly how I lived in the city. So I tried to concentrate on relaxing, and ate breakfast on the couch while I was watching the shadows the leaves made on the walls, like a puppet show. I have an overactive mind; the shadows soon drove me crazy. I read one of the paperbacks stacked on the bookshelf next to the wood stove, a ridiculous novel about a man who opens a restaurant in Colombia: cocaine and firearms, some kind of heist. It became too dark to read without turning on the light. I opened my second bottle of wine and drank it with the leftover pasta.

I don't know what time it was when I finally fell asleep, but I woke up on the couch shivering because the fire had gone out. I made myself a Go-Manchura drink before going upstairs to the bedroom. The tangerine flavour is the most refreshing—I keep packets of it in my purse just in case I need a lift. The next day I stayed in bed for hours and hours. My body must have needed the rest.

On Friday, they were due to arrive before sunset. I'd already defrosted a Go-Manchura ready-to-eat mushroom lasagna, and the ingredients for bruschetta and salad were ready. I selected three flower-remedy tinctures from the cabinet above the microwave: White Chestnut, for recurring thoughts; Impatiens, which is the obvious one; and Black Walnut, for the feeling of being stuck in a rut. The tinctures are made in a base of good brandy. I flavoured a glass of water with three drops from each vial and sipped it while standing at the kitchen sink, watching for a car to come up the hill. The water tasted sweet, like a glass of Scotch at the end of the night, when the ice has long since melted and it's time to go home.

The evening sun set the birch on fire, turned the chartreuse leaves electric. A sound like a seated lawnmower stewed at the bottom of the driveway. Then an old burgundy Volvo appeared all at once, taking the hill in a large mouthful. Nina and Brooks. The car hummed while Brooks fidgeted with the headlights and the parking brake. Nina's face looked eager, a sunflower pressed against the window. I drank the rest of my water, set the glass down on the counter, and walked out into the yellow leaves to greet them.

Nina looked amazing, as always. Hip-hugging red jeans—who else could wear red pants and pull it off?—with her little black boots that fold down, like a pirate's. She'd been wearing those boots when we did our Feldenkrais certification workshop years ago, long before they were popular. She slipped out of the passenger seat and stared straight up at the yellow birch trees with her hands on her hips. The one above the cottage was just turning: it had reached its apex of illuminated fluorescent insanity, and it would probably lose most of its leaves before the end of the weekend.

God, Nina said. It's like Pantone 803.

She turned back to the car and lugged a denim duffle bag out of the back seat. As she bent down to grasp the shoulder strap, her hair fell away from the back of her neck, showing her tattoo. In Gothic cursive, it read: *Earl Grey*. The Earl was Nina's old border collie, killed by a bear in a tree-planting camp ten years ago. I was with her when it happened. We weren't close enough to see it, but we heard it through the trees. Nina left the camp without finishing her contract and never returned to tree planting after that. She got a part-time job pulverizing carrots and apples at a juice bar, enrolled at the Ontario College of Art and Design, and starting painting with acrylics. She really got into the contact dance scene. That's how she found out about Feldenkrais. But this was all a long time ago. She's a web designer now. I think she's even started eating meat again, since she met Brooks.

I was so glad for the signs, said Brooks. I almost couldn't see the road because of all the leaves. Do they plough this in the winter?

Brooks is built tall and narrow, like a townhouse. I hugged him around the waist and my cheek could only reach the middle of his chest. He wore a thin black jacket that zipped up into a sleek tube. It was made of some kind of microfibre that was so soft and smooth, it had a negative texture.

We should go for a night walk tonight, I said to them. The leaves are falling constantly. It's so pretty, especially when it's dark.

You mean spooky, said Nina.

You can see the stars, I said.

I'm in! Brooks pumped his arm too vigorously. Nina rolled her eyes.

It's been a long time since we got Brooks out of the city, she said.

You both look so spiffy, I said.

I brought my new rubber boots, said Nina. I'm excited to be able to wear them.

Only two pairs of footwear this time? Brooks asked her. Well done!

Eight o'clock. Stephen and Evelyn still hadn't arrived. I made dinner anyway.

They'll want some when they get in, said Brooks.

They probably stopped at Arby's, said Nina.

Who eats at Arby's? I asked. I don't even know where to find an Arby's.

When you're looking for them, they appear, said Nina. It's sinister.

We were drinking homemade Chardonnay, care of Brooks's father. Nina had designed a series of labels for her father-in-law that read *Chateau Holland*, with an old picture of the family farm that she'd found at the archives. The wine itself was made at a brew-your-own franchise called The Cellar; the family farm had never grown any grapes. The land was now called Waverly Park, home to a new development of brick-veneer shoeboxes in the area north of Markham. Nina and Brooks had bought themselves a condo in the Argyle Lofts downtown. They bought it outright, as in: they have no mortgage.

I daubed a spoonful of walnut oil over the arugula and then sprinkled it with Go-Manchura's plum vinegar. When the pumpkin seeds started to pop in the cast iron pan, I slid them out onto a plate to cool. I diced tomatoes and piled them on top of the garlic bread.

Nina watched me screw the cap back on the purple bottle. What you got there? she asked.

It's one of the products I wanted to show you, I said. This vinegar improves digestion and discourages bacteria and yeast growth in the intestines.

Mm, said Brooks.

Nina peeked in at the lasagna and shut the oven door. And what's in there?

It's another one of these special products, I told her. The stuff I've been telling you about.

But what's it called? she asked.

It smells just great! said Brooks.

It's lasagna, I said.

Oh, said Brooks. That's funny, because it doesn't smell like lasagna.

All of the ingredients are certified organic, I said.

If I were to guess what it was, Brooks continued, I definitely wouldn't have said lasagna. I would have said—he closed his eyes and took a big whiff—mm, I would say more like beef stroganoff.

I hadn't tried this particular Go-Manchura entree yet, and I wanted it to be delicious. So much. I should have tested the mushroom one myself before serving it this weekend. I knew the Roast Veggies & Herb version was good, but I wanted to try something new. Stupid!

Yeah, I said, but no, it's lasagna.

Yeah no! said Nina. Notice how people from Toronto always say that? We always say that.

Say what? I asked.

Answer a question with yeah, no. It's a tic or something. Watch, you'll see.

Brooks lifted a bottle of Chateau Holland. More wine?

Yeah . . . no, I said.

That's it exactly, Nina said. I know you forced it that time, but still.

It did feel familiar coming off my tongue, I told her.

Nina smiled. That's right, she said. We do it all the time and we don't even notice.

Because it's a time-share and meant to be used by a number of families throughout one season, Cottage F (there are seven of them built around the lake, alphabetized from A to G) discourages any signs of character or human life. There are no old canoe paddles mounted over the fireplace, no smooth stones collected from the beach in a line on the windowsill, no blanket box full of faded quilts with the stitching coming undone from years of wear. The structure of the cottage is autonomous and self-satisfied. It merely tolerates human presence. It was built in a sturdy, present way: Large, blocky pine furniture with a golden varnish takes up space around the wood stove. A winding staircase to the second floor is almost in the centre of the living room. The floors are made of a matching yellow pine and waxed to a high, shiny finish. It's easy to slip if you are in sock feet. The steps used to be so slippery, the owners of the cottages had to sprinkle sand on the wet varnish to make traction. It feels like walking on an old emery board now.

We ate dinner around the dining room table behind the couch, close enough to the living room to watch the fire in the wood stove. It was already well past dark and still no Evelyn and Stephen.

I'm a little concerned, I said.

You know Evelyn, said Nina.

Have you two spent much time with this Stephen guy? I asked.

Brooks had used his knife to make a grid on the top of his lasagna, and he was cutting out square pieces, eating them one at a time. The shape of his lasagna on the plate was not unlike an oversized Tetris piece.

Brooks has, said Nina.

Brooks looked up, eyebrows raised. I've played squash with him, he said.

Wait—you work together, right? I asked. I couldn't remember how Evelyn had met Stephen. I thought that she'd worked with him, but then it came back to me—Brooks had set them up together.

We work on the same floor, Brooks said. We don't actually work on the same team.

Stephen's in legal services, whispered Nina.

Is he actually a lawyer? I asked.

Whatever, said Nina. He's loaded.

Is she happy with him?

Nina shrugged and pierced a grey wedge with the tines of her fork. I really like the mushrooms in here, she said. Is this shiitake?

Sometimes a portobello mushroom can taste just like a juicy steak, Brooks said.

Brooks proposed to Nina last November, on a weekend trip to Montreal. When they were settled in the hotel, a four-storey stone building in the old part of town, Nina asked him, Do you think we'll get married soon? Brooks brushed her off, so as not to ruin the surprise. Nah, he said, why rush it? Meanwhile, he had the ring in his pocket. Nina was so upset by his nonchalance, she locked herself in the bathroom, weeping. Brooks finally proposed to her on the other side of the bathroom door. She opened the door and saw him on one knee. He said, I didn't want to do it this way, but you're just so miserable.

Hey Brooks, I said. Do you know any other rich single men at your office?

Ha! Brooks laughed and nodded, like I'd made a great joke.

I'm serious, I said. Is there anyone?

There was a pause. Nina wrinkled her nose and tilted her head towards me. Lilian, she said, I don't think any of the guys in Brooks's office are really your type.

Why not? I asked.

Oh, you know, Nina said. You need someone who's more . . . She opened her hand in front of her as though making an offering. Conscious, she finished.

You found someone great, and he works in that office, I said to her.

Yes, but we're different, said Nina.

Who, you and Brooks?

You and me, she said.

I tried a bite of my lasagna. It wasn't too bad.

I'm exhausted, Nina said. She rested her fork on her plate, tines down. I might have to go to bed right after dinner. Lilian, do you have earplugs?

Not here, I said. Do you want to hear a little bit about Go-Manchura first?

Oh, I think it's too late tonight, she said. Maybe in the morning, we can have a little sit-down about it then? Do you mind?

The lasagna was very good, said Brooks. He'd finished his grid of a meal and folded his napkin in a tidy rectangle beside the plate.

I would love to tell you more about the health benefits, I said.

Nina nodded. If you crunch up toilet paper and lick it a little, she said, the paper will mould to the inside of your ear canal.

There are a few ways to sell the products: through friends, through strangers, and through turning strangers into friends. The Go-Manchura DVD promised that the easiest way to the path of health, wealth, happiness and success was by helping your friends first.

A slight tang pinched the air as I cleaned up after dinner: the vinegar from the salad, the leftover Chardonnay in the bottom of my guests' glasses. I hesitated before I drank their extra puddles of wine. I know it was a little unsanitary, but it wasn't like they were there to see it. They were upstairs having sex in the master bedroom. It was very loud: Nina called out like an exotic night bird from the Amazon.

I was dozing on the couch, the stumpy black bits in the wood stove still glowing cadmium, when I heard a long scratch at the door. I thought it was Evelyn. I didn't even think about why she'd be scratching instead of knocking. I froze when I opened the door, which was probably not the best reaction. There stood a black dog. It could have attacked me easily—I didn't even move, I just looked at it. It was a medium-sized dog that must have had some greyhound in it, because its face was long and pointy. The dog trotted in and immediately made for the braided rug that lay at the base of the wood stove. She turned in the three proverbial circles and exhaled a breath as she lay down. She had a very bushy tail, like a fox, and in less than a minute she'd inserted her nose deep into her fur, closed her eyes, and fallen asleep.

I began to feel anxious. But it was two-thirty in the morning; I couldn't call the caretaker of the cottages at that hour. I reasoned that she probably belonged to a time-share guest at one of the other cottages, obviously friendly, not dangerous. I fixed myself a Go-Manchura tangerine drink with several drops of the Aspen tincture, meant for vague and persistent fears, and settled myself back under the blanket on the couch. But I was far too uneasy to sleep in the presence of the dog. So I dropped a little shot of vodka in my drink to help me relax, and crept upstairs quietly, hoping she wouldn't follow me. She didn't. I slept in the bed I'd made up for Evelyn and Stephen. First thing in the morning, I would call someone.

It's just a nominal fee, I told Brooks. Then you get everything Go-Manchura makes at wholesale prices.

I was slicing the bread for toast, making a mess of the oats or kamut flakes or whatever it was that fell off the top of it, scattering onto the floor. Brooks was leaning against the counter, reading the fine print on the back of a Go-Manchura drink packet. He wore a bright orange sweater that looked lovely against the yellow birch leaves outside.

Is it a drug? he asked.

No, I told him. It's a mushroom. It's like a mushroom, but it's more complicated. It works like an herb. Like herbal medicine.

A flash of black ribbon came boiling through the door and into the kitchen, streaking around my legs, becoming canine as it slowed. Nina, layered in fleece and Gore-Tex, closed the door behind her. She unwound a long white scarf from her neck, looped it over a wooden peg next to the door, and turned to me, her pink cheeks shiny.

I can't believe I forgot my camera, she said. The frost is melting and all of the sparkles are turning to beads of water.

Toast? asked Brooks, holding up a slice in the air.

Nina dug off her rubber boots one heel at a time. Coffee! she said.

The dog was lying in front of the wood stove again, nibbling at her paws, pulling out weeds and burrs. I had called the caretaker's number, but she had an old message on her voice mail: it informed me that she would be away until one o'clock the previous Thursday. I had nothing to feed the dog, but then, she didn't seem hungry.

I have some Go-Manchura coffee I'd love for you to try, I said to Nina. I found the box inside the cupboard and slid three packets out. The kettle had been whistling just after Nina took the dog outside. It was still hot. It wouldn't take long to re-boil.

It's instant? said Nina.

Look, I said. It tastes so good, and it has much less caffeine than regular coffee.

Wait—it's decaf? said Brooks.

It's medicinal, I said.

The caretaker stood in the middle of our cabin, her hands stuffed tight in her jean pockets, and she shook her head. Wow, she said, that is a really cute dog.

Nina and Brooks had gone upstairs for a "nap" after breakfast, and I went down to the caretaker's cabin at the bottom of the hill to ask her about the dog. She had wanted to come back with me to see the dog herself. On the walk back up the hill, I caught myself doing that thing with my thumbs again—clenching them inside my fists and squeezing. But when I opened the door, the love circus had quieted. They may even have been sleeping.

I watched the dog lying by the fire. But where did she come from? I said. It's like she thinks she lives here.

The dog was watching us, eyes open, her nose pointed into the tail. The fur sprayed into her face and around her neck like a feather boa. She really did look elegant.

I haven't heard anything about a missing dog, said the caretaker. I could ask around town this afternoon.

Could you do that, please? I asked.

Evelyn's not coming, Nina called from upstairs. The caretaker jumped.

I didn't know you had company, she said.

They arrived last night, I said.

She just texted me, Nina called. She got some contract and can't leave the city.

I heard the water go on in the bathroom. Brooks cleared his throat in the glass shower stall and the echo sounded like an operatic barnyard animal.

Oh well! I shouted up the stairs. Thanks for telling me!

The dog raised her head at the noise and gave me a look.

Sorry, I said to her.

The caretaker turned to leave. I'll let you enjoy the rest of your weekend, she said.

Wait, I said. What should I do about the dog?

She shrugged. She looks fine, she said. I don't think you have to do anything.

Okay, yes, you can buy a similar ingredient at a health food store, I said to Brooks. He was lacing up his hiking boots by the door. Nina was standing beside him with her rubber boots already pulled up over the legs of her jeans. But, I continued, the thing about Go-Manchura is that it's certified organic, the ingredients are standardized, and the quality is guaranteed.

The dog had come into the kitchen to see what was going on. She sat down at Nina's feet and watched me with what I thought was a cool eye. Her tail brushed up into Brooks's bootlaces, and he pushed it away so he could see what he was doing.

Do they have a website? asked Brooks. He fitted a ribbed black hat onto his head and zipped up his tube jacket. The dog stood up, expecting to go for another walk.

I looked at the drink crystals, said Nina, and sugar is the first ingredient.

It's organic cane sugar, I said. It's unrefined and one hundred percent natural.

Nina folded her white scarf in half. She wrapped it around the back of her neck, slipped the two ends through the loop, and pulled it snug. The lasagna was good, she said.

Go-Manchura products are so restorative, I told them. You may feel a renewed amount of energy. Did you wake up feeling refreshed? I turned to Brooks. You can find them at Go-Manchura.com, I told him. But my client code number is 738.

Nina looked at me and sighed. What is this? she asked.

What do you mean? I said.

I think maybe I should just tell you straight up, Lilian. We're not interested.

I focused on the balls of fabric that had pilled on her scarf. The scarf was actually an oatmeal colour, not white at all. Her chin jabbed into the scarf like a chisel. Brooks stared down at the dog. The dog looked at something behind the door that none of us could see.

We think that this whole thing is kind of creepy, Nina said.

What Nina means is that this is probably not for us, said Brooks.

I wouldn't be telling you about these products unless I believed in them, I said. It's such a powerful ingredient. It's been proven to cure migraines.

Stop saying the word *products*, said Nina.

Do you know what the ingredient is? asked Brooks.

It's a pyramid scheme, said Nina.

It's like an ancient mushroom. But with a more complex biological structure.

A pyramid scheme that uses mushrooms for world domination! said Brooks.

Technically, it's not a mushroom, I corrected him.

After they left for their walk—all three of them, including the dog—I sat down at the kitchen table with my Go-Manchura portfolio, sales graph and marketing plan. The corporate philosophy is printed on the front cover of the portfolio:

> *Spiritual and financial wealth lead to a life of happiness and wholeness. At Go-Manchura, we strive to help you attain this. Success is possible when we attain our life objectives. We help you cultivate good leadership skills and improve your interpersonal communication skills, and through this you will find success. Our company creates a loving community that expands beyond the individual.*

Nina had left her pirate boots on the mat inside the door. One was standing exactly upright and the other was folded over, like a dog's ear. At that moment, I would have traded everything I had for those boots.

The dog and I had a photo shoot out in the leaves later that afternoon, while Brooks and Nina packed their things. I wanted to make a poster with pictures, to help find her owners. It was like she knew what it was, to pose for the camera. She sat on her butt, her tail flashing out behind her, and gave me her profile. I took a few shots of her walking towards me, her nose foreshortened in the lens, bulbous and gentle. I threw sticks for her and snapped shots when she was running back with the branch in her mouth, tongue flapping pink underneath it. I named her Friday, for the day she came to the door. I know it was a Saturday morning, technically, but Friday suited her personality. As soon as I named her, I knew that she'd probably leave.

At one point she looked back at the cottage, dropped her stick like a cold stone, and trotted to the door. She must have somehow heard the sound of Brooks and Nina coming downstairs with their luggage. She sat on her haunches, staring at the door, waiting for them to come outside. They packed their duffle bags back in the trunk of the Volvo, and Nina opened the back door to tuck her rubber boots behind the passenger seat. Friday, ready for exactly this moment, jumped in the car. She gave her usual smug and content expression: the sense of entitlement one is more accustomed to seeing in the face of a cat. I tried to get her out, calling her by her new name, as if she would recognize it. Brooks opened the door on the other side and gave her butt a push, but she step-danced all over the back seat, making it difficult for him to get a good angle. In the end, it was Nina who coaxed her out. She bent forward at the hip and patted her thighs, saying, Come. Come on, girl. Out.

Friday listened to every word she said. She calmly stepped out of the car because Nina had asked her to do it.

Nina spread out her arms for me, and I hugged her. It felt like embracing a sheet of vellum. Brooks touched the top of my head. I smiled brightly, as though he'd knighted me.

Goodbye, Lilian, he said.

I stood behind the Volvo as Brooks made a six-point turn in the small driveway. He watched me in his mirrors and I used my hands to signal where the tree trunks were, and called out that it was safe to keep coming, keep coming, a little more, now stop. Okay, now you can go.

Friday and I both stood in the driveway for a while, long after the Volvo's tail lights had disappeared beyond the hill, long after I stopped hearing the engine humming down the gravel road. Friday's ears were up, full triangles. Her tail was at rest, but poised for action. She stared deep into the distance, as if she could see beyond the trees and the leaves, as if she could still see them in the car, even though they were long gone.

Oh, go on, I said. Just go.

Standing Up

for Janey

Janey stands on a wooden platform in front of three angled mirrors, twisting so she can see how the dress looks from the back. There are a hundred little covered buttons running up her spine. The silk straps are too long for her. They wilt off her shoulders. The attendant nips them with two pinched fingers. We can fix those, she says. Don't worry about the straps.

Janey catches my eye in the centre mirror. You're supposed to cry when you see me try it on, she says. That's how I'll know it's the right one.

I turn my head sideways and blink a few times.

Stop faking it, Janey says.

Let's try it with the veil, the attendant says, then rustles off.

When we're alone in the dressing room, I say, You're joking, right?

Janey looks at her reflection. Yes, she says, talking to the mirror, I'm joking. She pokes one foot out from under the hem, holding her skirt, pointing her toes like a dancer. A long white thread hangs from the seam of the bodice. I want to tug at it, but I'm afraid it might make the whole dress unravel.

I like it, I tell her. It's simple. Classic.

Janey reaches into the front of the dress and lifts her left breast so it rests properly in the cup. Then she shimmies both breasts closer together to make more cleavage.

All brides think they have simple gowns, she says. Ask anyone who's been married. She'll say, My dress was very simple.

I watch Janey's reflection. It's like I've been watching her in a mirror ever since the engagement. My response wavers like a needle on a polygraph: dopey joy, strange feeling of dread. I have always felt suspicious of weddings. But I'm her maid of honour. There are these shots of anxiety in my chest that I can't explain.

This isn't a simple dress, Janey says to me in the mirror. The buttons alone make it complicated.

Janey and Milt were going to have a potluck at the YMCA Community Room. The plan was: a simple wraparound skirt and whatever flowers were in season. Milt's band would play after they said their vows. But then Janey booked a priest at St. Anthony's and talked Milt into platinum wedding bands. Milt is a high school teacher trying to save up for a used Toyota, and Janey hasn't even found herself a job yet. Something from Birks, she told him. We should have something in a little blue box. These are the rituals we have in North America.

Three weeks later, back at my place, Janey sits in the living room playing with her pack of cigarettes, trying not to smoke them. She has something to say. I'm in the kitchen breaking garlic cloves apart, arranging them on the tray for the toaster oven. I'm charring red peppers in the big oven. I've placed a bowl of fat green olives on the table, and a loaf of Calabrese bread with my good knife stuck in it. Milt and his sister are coming over in about an hour. I'm making dinner for all of us tonight. Except David. I haven't seen him since he moved out of our apartment six weeks ago. What's the rule about getting over a breakup? Does it take twice as much time as the length of the relationship, or half as much time? It has to be half. I can't spend ten years feeling like this.

My cat, Timotei, slinks around the corner and sticks her chin up at me. She smells the olives. When she was a kitten, I would find her on the pantry shelf licking the cap from the olive oil bottle. David trained her to stop that with a blue plastic water pistol. She'd never jump on the shelf now. But she still loves olives. I pinch one from the dish, pop it in my mouth, and bend down to let her lick my outstretched finger. Her tongue is pink and serrated.

The school just asked Milt to be the wrestling coach. Janey says he's excited. Deep inside the heart of every man, she told me, there is a boy who loves to wrestle. But

I just can't picture it. I keep thinking of Milt yelling at a pile of boys squatting and wriggling over each other in the gymnasium. Then I think of Milt playing mandolin at the Teahouse Café every Friday night. David would tell me that people contradict themselves, that this is what makes us human, and that I have to learn to tolerate it. And he's right. I should enjoy our contradictions. I slip the tray of garlic cloves into the little oven and turn the knob to max.

David forgot a whole case of his special Chianti when he moved out. It's a vintage he ordered direct from Italy from Wine Online. He hoarded the wine for so long, waiting for an occasion that was special enough to drink it. And then, impossibly, he abandoned it. Sometimes, despite myself—usually late at night when I can't sleep and my spirit is weak—I'll open the cabinet door just to look at the twelve dark, moody bottles.

When I invited him to come to dinner tonight, he said, You know that's a bad idea, Bonnie. But David should be here tonight, he really should. I mean, for Janey and Milt.

I ceremoniously take the middle one out of the top row. The label is gold, like the inside wrapper of a good bar of chocolate. An embossed image of an old castle. Too ostentatious for my taste. This wine is ten years old already.

Bonnie, come in here and keep me company, Janey calls to me.

I pull the cork with my eyes closed like I'm making a wish.

Everything's done, I say, coming out with two glasses.

She's stretched out on the couch, barefoot. When did they say they'd get here?

We have lots of time, I say. I find myself a spot on the floor. Now, you tell me.

She reaches for the wine. First, you have to promise.

There's a collection of cat hair underneath the couch. I don't usually see the couch from this angle. I resist the urge to get up and vacuum before Milt and his sister get here.

Becky makes me nervous, I say. Does she seem uptight to you?

Becky was raised by her grandmother, she tells me. But she's fine.

Who raised Milt?

Janey curls her toes over the arm of the couch. His dad came back when he was a kid, she says. But his grandmother took care of him too, I guess. Still lying down, she twists her hair with one finger and holds her wine in the other hand. The glass teeters and I'm afraid she's going to spill it.

You're lucky that Milt is so laid-back, I say. David could be so uptight.

Janey says, I saw David last night. He's still uptight.

I watch Janey's wineglass. Where? I try to sound nonchalant.

Do you really want to hear this? Janey says. Should I be telling you this?

Was he with someone?

He was with us.

Timotei has coiled herself around the corner and into the living room. She finds me on the floor and dives headfirst into the carpet at my feet, then wriggles onto her back, asking for a rub.

I'm fine, I say, though I feel a lick of fear in my belly. The truth is that I'm relieved to not be with David anymore. I didn't trust him when he lived with me. But the problem is, now he's gone and I still don't trust him. I know it's none of my business whom he's drinking with at

Legends. I know I have to let go.

Tell me the story, I say to Janey.

Well, you know how Legends is so awful, Janey says. I mean, I won't even drink anything out of a glass there. Have you ever held a Legends glass up to the light? So poor David, he's trying to order a nice glass of wine. Who drinks wine at Legends? I kept telling him, Just get a beer, just get a beer.

She laughs and takes a sip of the Chianti. Now this is nice wine, she says.

It's David's, I tell her. He forgot about a case of this in the closet when he left.

It's quiet for a minute. The red peppers sizzle in the oven. I rub my hand over Timotei's belly, those little pink nubs buried in silver fur.

What did you want me to promise? I ask.

That you'll always be my best friend, she says.

I've missed my chance. Whatever it was, she's not going to tell me now. I brought a kind of cancer into our conversation by saying the words *when he left*. But the air around Janey still shimmers. She looks like she's just fallen in love.

Are you whitening your teeth? I ask.

Janey sits up on the couch, sets her wineglass down on the coffee table, and stares at me. Her skin smooth and holy like scrubbed stone.

To make her laugh again, I say, You're not screwing around with anyone, are you?

She puts her hand up to her mouth. I can't believe it, she says. Why would you ask me that?

Janey is still wearing that silver bracelet with the hummingbird engraved in the band. It's a Haida design. I found it for her in Vancouver, before we ever met these men. I gave it to her as a coming-off-antidepressants gift. She went off the Paxil too quickly, though, and relapsed into an even worse depression soon after I gave it to her.

I moved into her little West End apartment with the Murphy bed that I pushed back into the wall each morning. We smoked Nat Shermans out on the fire escape and listened to Buddhist meditation tapes. When a thought appears in your mind, the monk told us, imagine it as a soap bubble, and push it away with a feather.

I used a small scalpel blade to shave tiny piles of powder from the blue pills, measuring minuscule amounts so she could come off gradually. It took over a month, but she hasn't been on them since, as far as I know. Not counting the occasional Xanax before bed, or Ativan for the plane.

I was just joking, I say to her. I focus on her wrist when I say this. I wasn't seriously suggesting it.

The bones in Janey's wrists are very fine. There are pale blue veins just under the surface. Janey has always looked lovely in blue. It occurs to me that this could be because of her thin skin.

It's not obvious, then? she asks.

I look up at her.

I told him that it had to stop, she says. She drops her hand to my ponytail and loosens the elastic. Let me play with your hair. When was the last time someone played with your hair?

She sifts strands of my hair through her fingers. My shoulders have been perched up around my ears all day. Her nails trace fine lines through my roots, like the long toothpicks they used to check for lice in grade school. I close my eyes, absorb the shiver.

Wait, I say. You still want to get married, right?

Yes. Of course. He was—This wasn't like that. It was just something I needed to do before the wedding.

I love Milt, I say. Milt is good.

Milt is good, she agrees.

The wineglass feels cool in my hand. I'm surprised by Janey's affair, but not shocked. She's been so remote. I want to press her for details, but I'm cautious.

We assume love is singular, Janey says. She's making a braid now. That it's exclusive. Why do we do that?

Chemistry, I tell her. It's chemistry you're talking about.

Maybe, she says. Maybe chemistry regulates love.

Love is a decision, I say.

If love is a decision, and there's no magic meant-to-be, then it's just arbitrary, isn't it? We could just be with anyone.

I pull away from Janey's hands. I stand up and look at her. She's sitting cross-legged on the couch, the way we used to sit when we were meditating.

Do you love this guy? I ask.

She puts her hands to her face. I think so, she says. Bonnie, I feel a little out of control.

And I can see it there inside her, the squirm of serotonin, the flush in her cheeks. I cross my arms and nod my head, aware that it makes me look more judgmental than I actually feel. Well this explains it, then, I say. The white dress. The platinum wedding bands.

I was always going to be an ironic bride, Janey says.

I manage to say, You look great, Milt, and hold my cheek up when he gives me a kiss in the doorway. He has showered recently, and I smell something herbal when he comes close, like rosemary, or marijuana. Behind him, Becky gives my hallway an appraising look.

Thanks for doing this, Milt says.

It's my pleasure, I say. I'm so happy you're here.

No, I mean, we appreciate what you're doing tonight.

Oh, it's nothing, I say, flinging my hand. I love this, I love having you. I can't look into Milt's open face for longer than a couple of seconds. His big eyes, his wide mouth. When he smiles, it's like he's throwing open a set of double doors so you can step out onto the veranda.

It smells wonderful in here, Becky says to me. She's wearing a gold Thai silk scarf. It makes her hazel eyes look yellow.

It's the garlic, I tell her, and run into the kitchen.

Is she okay? I hear Becky ask Janey. I don't hear the reply, because as soon as I reach the kitchen, something explodes inside the toaster oven.

I come back out, unharmed, with glasses of Chianti for Becky and Milt.

One of my garlics popped, I tell them. I try to say this calmly, but I don't know if I pull it off. I hand them each a glass. I was roasting garlic, I add, unnecessarily.

You're supposed to wrap the whole bulb in tinfoil, Becky tells me. To protect the cloves.

Aha, I murmur into my glass.

Becky is an installation artist. Her last show involved fibre optic cables and old letters from her great-grandparents. I think she wove the wires through the letters, making some kind of light-blanket. Janey told me that Becky is an extraordinary grant writer. She's shown her work in Berlin and New York City. I wish I knew more about her work. I should have Googled her before she arrived.

Janey holds on to Milt's arm like it's a tree trunk.

God, you're beautiful, he says. Bonnie, isn't Janey beautiful?

She's gorgeous, I say.

Janey covers her face with one hand. Stop it, she says. You guys.

Becky goes into the kitchen to inspect the damage for herself. She'll see my mess: The cutting board with the core of red pepper on it, all the seeds. Papery skins from the garlic bulbs, fragrant and unmanageable.

Please, I say to Milt. Have something to eat.

Janey pulls him to the table and slips an olive into his mouth. He nips at her fingertips with his teeth like a goat at the petting zoo, making her squeal and pull away, feigning injury with a pout.

Becky comes out of the kitchen and goes straight to the bread on the table. I found a marvellous balsamic at Olivieri's last week, she tells me. She tugs at the knife to pull it out. Aged, she murmurs. It pours like a syrup.

I like Olivieri's, I say, and try to think of a good reason for saying this. I add: Their cheeses.

Don't you just? she responds, ripping a small piece of bread off the loaf.

I've forgotten to put on music. The sound of everyone eating and swallowing. There's a smudge of flour on the corner of Becky's mouth.

Is this *levain* bread? she asks. It has a perfect crumb.

I have a compilation disc that I know Janey likes. I go to the bookshelf by the window to find the CD, but Milt beats me to it. He pulls my stereo out from the wall so he can see the cords in the back. With two gentle yanks, he disconnects my speakers. Then he attaches another cord—this one connected to his cellphone. His index finger touches the screen and the device makes clicking insect noises as he looks for what he wants. He chooses an old Miles Davis album.

David bought the same album for me years ago. It sounds like our first apartment. It was so drafty we had to buy sheets of plastic for the storm windows and seal them to the edges with a hair dryer. Then Timotei sliced the plastic with her claws three days after we put it up. David tried to fix the cuts instead of buying another package of plastic sheeting. As though Scotch tape could keep the draft out.

He's obsessed with his new toy, Janey says. It knows how to tell you what music is playing, anywhere you hear music. You hold it up in a bar, it listens, and then it tells you what the song is, what album, everything. Press a button and you can buy the song, right there. She's back on the couch, sitting up straight, finger combing her hair. Milt, can you put something else on?

Becky has moved over to the olives. I scan the table quickly to see if I've remembered to put out a dish for the pits, which I have. I zip into the kitchen to check on the sauce.

Becky follows me. Do you mind if I have a taste? she asks. She's come prepared, with a crust of bread in her hand.

I nod to the saucepan on the stove. Tell me what you think.

She lifts the lid and moves to avoid the steam, then pokes her face in. Mmm, she says, and dips in a corner of bread. I've laced the sauce with red wine and baby clams. I've tied a bunch of thyme together with string, it's been in there all afternoon.

Nice and herby, she says. Bonnie—can I ask you?

It's thyme, I tell her.

She looks at me intently, her forehead wrinkled. I can tell that she's misunderstood my response. Her lipstick has worn off. There's a plum-coloured line left on her top lip, drawn carefully, the top of a heart.

I don't want to have this conversation. I turn away from her and look for something to stir the sauce. I think this is just about ready, I say.

The sauce makes little bubbles of itself and each one splatters with a breathy pop. The stovetop is sprinkled with drops of sauce. It's been simmering for a long time.

I turn off the heat. Becky is quiet, watching me.

Then she asks, What do you think Janey wants?

This surprises me. I thought it was obvious: Janey wants to be married. She wants to have a job that makes her happy and a house of her own. She wants a husband who's not afraid to kiss her in public, who will volunteer to light the barbecue and fix the plugged drain. Soon she will want to have a baby.

Janey wants to be loved, I say. Just like we all do.

Becky nods slowly, still looking down at the saucepan. You understand that I'm simply concerned about Milton. He's more sensitive than he lets on.

I fill a second pot with water and sprinkle some salt in it, turn the burner up to high and look on the counter for the lid.

They're getting married because they love each other, I say.

I would hate to see him get hurt, Becky says.

I can't find the lid. The water will never boil without it. I find a plate and rest it on top of the pot instead. The salad is ready. We can just start with salad.

Janey has a good heart, I tell her. Nobody's going to get hurt. I try to smile. I reach for the salad bowl and hold it with both hands. Do you mind bringing in the pepper mill? I motion to the wooden club standing beside the toaster oven.

Listen to me. Becky moves her body so it blocks my passage to the living room. She's had her eyebrows shaped into two isosceles triangles. Her face is like an arrow pointing right through me.

She says, Your good-hearted Janey told my little brother that he had to spend three thousand dollars on each wedding band. Don't try to tell me this is simply about love.

I exhale. Okay, I tell her, I don't know what's going on with Janey. It looks like she caught the wedding bug. I haven't been able to talk to her about it. She's just obsessed with everything bridal right now. I eye the pepper mill on the counter.

Becky follows my gaze, sighs, and reaches for it. It was my mother's pepper mill, handmade. There is a small flower design carved in a ring around the middle of it.

Milt told me about your broken engagement, Becky says. I want to say that I think it's admirable. I mean, I respect what you're doing here. To wear the brave face, making us dinner tonight, handling the rehearsal dinner as well, the wedding cake, everything. You must feel resentful about their wedding, though. I understand.

I don't feel resentful, I say.

Because it would be only natural for you to want to see another relationship fall apart right now. It can be very threatening to spend time with a couple when you know that your own relationship was a failure.

I take a breath and do that thing that David taught me to do whenever I feel angry with someone: I try to imagine Becky as a child. I really try to do this. I look down and imagine that I'm looking at a small version of the woman in front of me. I say to this little girl inside my head, I know that things didn't go well for you. I know that your mother died and your father went away to India because he was so sad, and I'm sorry that your bossy Ukrainian grandmother made you eat unfamiliar food and wear homemade dresses. But mostly I say to this little girl, I am sorry that you turned into such an unpleasant, spiteful woman.

So, Milt says when we come out of the kitchen. He grips the stem of his wineglass like it's a squash racquet. How's it going in there?

There's a strange voice coming from the stereo. Deep and unwavering, a voice like fruit soaked in liquor. I look at Janey on the couch. Her eyes are closed and her body seems loosened, relaxed, possibly drunk.

Who's this? I ask.

Local guy, says Milt. Singer-songwriter who's been playing the circuit up and down the Island. He raises his shoulders in a shrug and drinks a gulp. Goes by his last name, Rastin. Janey's gone to see him play a few times.

He calls himself Rasputin? says Becky.

Rastin, says Milt. Not Rasputin.

I've misplaced my wineglass. I spot one on the coffee table and move the salad bowl under my arm so I have a free hand to pick up the glass. I shouldn't be drinking more wine; I already feel clumsy. I want everyone to go home.

Janey opens her eyes. She smiles at me, one arm wrapped around herself in a half hug. Are we ready? she says.

When Janey was six years old, her father was hospitalized for mononucleosis. Something went wrong in the hospital. The mono turned into pneumonia and he died. I don't know all of the details. I doubt that Janey knows them herself. After he died, Janey and her brother went to a neighbour's house to spend the night. The neighbour baked a cake for the two children. It was a yellow cake with chocolate icing. When they tried to slice it, it crumbled everywhere, all over the table, like a fallen sandcastle. Her brother made up a song. He started singing, Messy cake, messy cake! Janey remembers laughing until they were screaming and crying, running around the table at this nice neighbour's house, yelling a song about cake at the top of their lungs because it was the only thing they could make themselves cry about.

I'm making Janey and Milt's wedding cake. It's going to be coconut with vanilla buttercream frosting. There won't be any chocolate. I won't even make a lemon cake because I am afraid to make the batter yellow, afraid to trigger the memory. I don't want to see their relationship fail. I love Janey and Milt. I want this to work for them.

Come and eat, babe, I tell Janey.

Becky, subdued from carbohydrates, sits down first. She glances at the slices of roasted red peppers, which I've peeled and arranged on a plate and drizzled with oil. They look obscene now, like tongues. I stand uselessly at the head of the table. Milt has turned the volume down, but he hasn't changed the music. Janey is still looking at me with that half smile on her face. I can't meet her eye. I put the salad bowl down on the table. I use a pair of wooden spoons to place shining bunches of green leaves on their side plates, as though each offering is a prayer.

David has been drinking. He's at the door wearing his blue snowboarder hat and the tacky fleece scarf that he got as a freebie at the wine store last winter. A bunch of grapes embroidered in cheap gold thread with *Cherry Pointe Vineyards* in cursive stitching at the bottom. As soon as I see him, I remember why I don't want him in my life.

I heard there was a party happening, he says. I heard that this is where it was all going down tonight.

You were invited, I tell him quietly. You said it would be a bad idea.

Bonnie, Bonnie! He holds his chest with one hand, pretending that he's been stabbed, and staggers a few feet back. He holds on to the door frame with his other hand and pulls his face in close to mine. Bonnie, he says, you're killing me.

Who is it? Janey calls from the living room.

Please can I come over for dinner? he asks in a high voice. Please?

Timotei is rubbing herself against David, winding herself between his ankles. She's happy that he's come back. She pushes the side of her face against his leg, rubbing each side over and over, as though she wants to wear through the corduroy.

You could have called first, I say. He walks past me and hangs his coat up on the hook that he drilled into the wall. When he raises his arm, his bicep pushes against the cuff of his T-shirt. I close the door behind him.

It's in a jar of formaldehyde, Janey is saying. Like twelve inches. It's on display in a Russian museum.

So that's why he's Russia's greatest love machine, says Milt.

Well, well, look who's here, says Janey.

If it isn't Miss Janey Brown, David says, holding his arms out for a hug. Give us a kiss, baby.

Janey stands up when David hugs her. Watching David touch Janey used to make me feel cramps of jealousy, but I made myself get over it. This is the first time I've seen them together since we broke up. There's a new cramp now, an unnamed feeling. Milt gets up too, puts his hand on David's back. I didn't think you could make it tonight, he says.

David is still wearing his blue hat. Change of plans, he grins.

Well, it's good to see you, man.

There's something stuck in my molar. A piece of walnut from the salad. I am aware that I'm distorting my face when I move my jaw to the side and let my tongue fish around for the offending crumb in my tooth. I leave them to it at the table and go into the kitchen so I can jam my finger back there and dig it out.

I say to everyone, I'm just going to get another bottle of that wine.

Let me help you, David says.

I can do it.

I need a glass, he says.

I'll get you a glass.

Oh, let her get it, says Janey. You have to tell us about the kayaking place. We might do that for our honeymoon. We might find a little lodge and learn how to kayak, and you're the perfect person to talk to about that. What do you think? Do you think I could do it, David?

I stop listening once I find myself in the kitchen. I crouch down and open the lower cabinet and stare at the eleven remaining wine bottles lined up on their sides in the rack that David built to fit the cupboard. The bottle necks point out at me like long snouts. I pick at my back tooth with my forefinger but can't find whatever has lodged itself in there. I take my finger out and try my teeth again. It feels like I'm biting on a chunk of granite.

David and Janey used to love each other. They lived together for a handful of years and then David met me and things changed. David and I were good together. He used to say that being with me felt like coming home. I want to tell everyone at the dinner table: You can't trust love. Everything changes eventually. Don't try to cement something just because you're afraid you're going to lose it.

My Chianti! says David. He's crouched behind me.

Um, I say. I've just got something stuck in my tooth.

Let me see it.

No.

Let me see.

His hands touch my shoulders.

This is weird, he says.

What part?

I don't know if I'm happy for them. I don't think I am.

Does it really matter if you are or aren't?

Are you happy for them?

Look, I just need some dental floss.

Bonnie, okay. I need to tell you something.

Don't.

Let me say it.

I interrupt him: Janey has a lover.

What?

Janey's been sleeping with someone. Milt doesn't know.

His body falls backwards, like he's lost his balance.

The music that's playing right now. The guitarist.

David clears his throat. You're saying Janey's sleeping with Rastin?

I just found out.

Janey told you that?

Help me with this, I tell him. Get the corkscrew.

The pasta is finally ready and I serve it to everyone in generous bowls with fresh curls of Parmesan on top. David put together an extra place setting for himself and he's squished in between Becky and Janey, at the corner of the table. Timotei is sleeping on the couch in the living room. I take this as a sign that the atmosphere is peaceful.

I've been saving this wine for a special occasion, David says. And tonight is the night. He raises his glass. To Janey and Milt, he says.

David makes sure that each person at the table meets his eye as he clinks his glass to each of theirs. This is what David does at dinner parties. He moves his glass from person to person purposefully. He raises his eyebrows and makes his eyes widen, looking for each glance before he moves on. He looks deranged as he does this.

So, Janey says, using her spoon to coax her noodles onto the fork, what are you working on these days, Becky? Any shows coming up?

I'm working with sugar syrup, she says. It's not like anything I've used before—I've had to talk to candy manufacturers to find out how I'm supposed to use it. I'm making a—yes—well, a sculptural work.

She made a body cast out of plaster, says Milt.

Whose body? I ask.

My own body, she says.

I laugh before I can stop myself. But it's unsophisticated to laugh at contemporary art, so I correct myself and say: Oh, goody! A life-sized Becky candy! What flavour will you be?

I'm glad you asked me that, Becky says. She nods her head, letting her fork dangle from her fingers like a pendulum over the bowl of pasta. Choosing a flavour, she tells me, will authenticate the project more than any other aspect of the composition. I had considered using cherry—but then, that's so obvious, isn't it?

Not that anyone would be tasting it, says Milt. Am I right?

That's part of the joy of installation work, Becky tells him with one eyebrow raised to a point. You never know how people will respond. Then she rolls her eyes and puts her fork down. God, it was hellish, she says. I had my students make the body cast, but they worked from the top down instead of up from my feet, so not only was my face encased in plaster for five hours while they covered my legs, but the weight of the plaster as I stood there—it dried on my body, it took hours—well, I think the weight of it did something to my back. I haven't felt the same since that session. And since my shiatsu therapist decided to change her name to Pashmina and sail to Maui, I'm just caught in this chronic pain cycle.

I have a massage therapist, I say. I have her card, remind me, I'll give it to you.

I'm sorry, Bonnie, I mean, I'm sure your massage therapist is lovely for you. But regular massage doesn't work *for me*. I have a certain constitution that responds to the energetic approach of shiatsu.

Pashmina? asks David. Really? Isn't that a scarf?

I don't know, says Becky. Her name used to be Margaret, and all I know is that she's gone now, and I'm in pain.

It's a wool wrap, says Janey. I'm wearing one in lavender, for the wedding.

You could carry lavender, I say. To make it all go together.

It's not the season for it, Becky says. And dried flowers are terrible feng shui. You don't want dried flowers in a wedding. You want fresh everything.

Because a wedding is a fresh start, says David.

I shoot him a look over the table.

Speaking of fresh starts, says Milt, what's up with Mr. Pressman, Beck?

I watch Milt use his knife to slip some noodles onto the edge of his fork—he's cut the noodles with the knife, he's cut them into small pieces—and a warm punch of love for him hits my chest. Janey is lucky to have found Milt. She asks too much from him, but he gives it anyway, and it pleases him to please her.

Becky says, Mr. Bradley Pressman, professional scoundrel, is up to no good. She holds her wineglass up like she is waving a flag. I have tried to avoid him, but he insists on showing up at every single opening I've been to this month. If I didn't know better, I'd say he was stalking me.

Isn't that a good thing? asks Janey. Doesn't he own Pressman Gallery?

He does, says Becky. He and Mrs. Pressman own the gallery.

Aha, says David. The wife.

That's right, says Becky. And his hands had no business being where they were, at the opening of Hirakawa's show last week. For example.

He touched you? asks Janey. How? Where were his hands?

Where was his wife, I want to know.

You don't know what kind of relationship they have, says David.

I look at him. What does that mean? I ask.

Well, they could have an arrangement.

Janey says, Maybe she has a whole collection of lovers, herself. They could have talked about it, about finding a little something on the side. Maybe it spices up their own sex life.

I say, So he's hitting on Becky, his wife knows about it, and she's okay with it.

It's a theory, says David. Just a theory. Affairs happen.

Milt says, Is it an affair if the wife knows about it?

No, I say. It's only an affair if it's a secret. That damn kernel of something is still stuck in my tooth. I can't stick my finger in my mouth again. I drink more wine, swirl it around to distract myself from the discomfort. I watch Janey across from me. One of her hands is under the table, likely on Milt's knee.

Well, it couldn't be a secret, Becky says, because he's not hiding his affections.

Has he asked to see your work? asks David.

Yes, she says. And I haven't shown it to him. I don't want to charm my way into the gallery just because he likes to see me at these openings in heels and silk. I want to earn it the proper way. The real way.

What's real anymore? I say. Nothing's real.

This causes a bit of a silence. Janey is watching me now.

Milt says, Uh. He's looking down onto his plate. I found something, he says. I don't know what this is, but it looks important.

He pokes into his dish and pulls out a black, matted clump that hangs like a tumour from the tines of his fork.

It's the thyme, I tell him. You're the lucky one, you got it on your plate. You get to make a wish.

You want me to wish on this? He makes a face.

I thought that only happened with wishbones, says David.

Oh, shut up, I tell him. You're just jealous. Milt got the thyme, he gets the wish.

Do I have to keep it a secret? Milt asks.

I give up and dig my index finger into my mouth, searching for the seed or whatever it is that has wedged itself into my tooth. Thorry, I mumble, I have this thing thuck in my thooth. Excuth me.

From across the table, I watch Janey's eyes fill with water when she looks at me. Milt doesn't notice that Janey's crying, but David does. He rubs her shoulder with one slow hand. He presses his hand to the base of her neck with care, like he's lining up the bones in his fingers with her vertebrae to see if they match. I can't stop watching them. My finger is still stuck in my mouth and I drool onto my wrist, just like a baby.

Where Are You Coming From, Sweetheart?

On the night her father died, Christine was in the dark of a Greyhound bus on the way from the Big Smoke to the Big Nickel, in one of the rear seats beside the washroom stall, letting a man named Bruce Corbiere put his smoky, apple-sticky tongue in her mouth. It felt like a living thing, burrowing. This was Christine's first kiss. She was fourteen years old.

Christine's father had allowed her to spend the weekend with her cousin Sonia and her aunt Juicy in Mississauga. The Greyhound bus was headed back north on Highway 69, the same stretch of road that had taken her own mother ten years earlier. Christine had been four years old, pencilling lumpy butterflies on the back of a phone bill envelope, when a police officer knocked at the door to report the accident. Christine's mother was driving the silver Valiant home from her sister's house when a transport truck swerved into oncoming traffic. It crushed the car and trapped her mother inside. This happened so long ago, it's more story than memory. She knew the detail about the butterflies on the envelope because her father still used this piece of paper as a bookmark in the black leather bible next to his bed.

Before she left for the weekend, Christine had had to finish all of her household chores—her father used the word *chores*, as if they lived on a farm. She was in the basement on Wednesday after school, cramming her father's brown pants into the washing machine, when she found the note. She had dipped into his pockets looking for money. The pocket lining was dotted with pimples of

pilled cotton. She pulled out a crusty handkerchief and a fat beige crumb of—what? It was heavy as a pebble, disgusting. But in the other pocket there was a scrap of paper, folded twice. *42:1–11 My tears have been my food day and night. Why are you downcast, O my soul? Put your hope in God.* The handwriting was dark and loopy. She threw it away, into the can of dryer lint with the dead house centipedes. Not even a quarter.

While her father boiled sausages with onions in the kitchen—Christine wouldn't eat this anymore because she was a vegetarian—Christine vacuumed his bedroom. He had been home from work all week because of a bad headache. She used the corner attachment to suck up the flakes of cigarette ash along the baseboards, picked up the empty soup bowls and pop cans that had rolled under the bed. She wiped the dandruff off the top of the headboard with a damp cloth and emptied her father's ashtray where it sat beside his bible.

Because she went into his bedroom every week, she knew: her father's closet was still full of her mother's old clothes. And he moved them around. He touched them. One day she found a peach polyester nightie crumpled in the bed. The whole scene was too revolting to contemplate—her father's hairy arms twisting the nightie into a thick cord, a sash, dangling it over his face, squeezing it, oh, horrible, slipping it between his legs? Christine had stripped the bed, thrown the nightie in with the rest of the load, and hung it up on a wire hanger in the very back of the closet. This Wednesday, thankfully, there was nothing unexpected in there. She changed the sheets on his bed, added the dirty ones to the laundry basket, and brought the basket down to the basement for a second load.

After dinner, Christine had asked her father if she could watch an episode of *Lost and Gone*. Sean Paisley played the doctor's younger brother and he was in the whole second season. He was without question the most adorable boy on television. She had rented the DVD from Video 99 three days ago. It was only a three-day rental.

Lost and gone, her father said, his hands folded in his lap. His blue jogging pants ballooned around his skinny legs and the ankle elastics made the jersey pouf over the top of his slippers. Are you lost and gone too, Christine?

She daubed dish detergent in the bottom of the greasy sausage pot and turned on the hot water. She dropped their two knives and two forks into the suds, one by one. Her father always sat at the kitchen table after dinner to watch her clean up.

No, Christine said. It's just a show, okay?

Her father stared at the running water. The Bible tells us to be filled with joy and praise, he said.

Christine turned off the tap and reached for the sponge. Amen amen amen amen hallelujah praise the lord, she said.

Her father sighed and let out an invisible cloud of suffering. I try to teach you the Right Way, he said. But I have failed. He pushed the palms of his hands into his eyes.

Take an Aspirin or something, Christine said. You are so full of negativity.

I'd like to call a house meeting, her father said, his eyes still covered. Meet me in the living room when you're finished. He stood up and shuffled out of the kitchen. Christine swiped the knives and forks with the soapy sponge and rinsed them under hot water.

It's not like we're poor, Christine told him. You work for the government.

We aren't rich, he said. He was sitting in the brown chair in the living room with the Household Debt ledger book open on his lap. Columns of numbers stumbled over the lines in blue ballpoint. This book tracked Christine's spending habits.

I take issue with this, Christine said.

We'll mark it in the book.

I don't have ten dollars for you, Christine said. I owe you everything already.

Thirty-five for the bus tickets, he said, writing in the book, plus ten dollars standard for the visit. He traced his finger down the Debt column. Three hundred twelve dollars, he said, making a note in blue pen.

If I'm paying for the tickets, how is it fair that I have to pay you ten dollars extra?

Nobody ever said life was fair, he said.

You are such a cliché.

Do you want to take the trip or not?

Christine stared at the top corner of the notebook, at the silver coils ridging down the side. They started to vibrate like an optical puzzle. Look closely: are the lines straight or curved? She closed her eyes and watched the yellow shapes float on the black of her eyelids. Just put it on my tab, she said, eyes closed.

You get one dollar for doing the dishes tonight, her father said.

Awesome.

And four dollars from Sunday.

Christine opened her eyes and tapped the plastic DVD case on her thigh.

So that's three hundred seven, he said, and drew a line in the book.

Last Sunday after church, they had driven out to the lake to collect empty beer bottles from the bush parties. Her father wore the Beer Bag, a top-loader backpack that was so stained and filthy it made their whole garage smell like sour fruit and rotten cheese. Christine had to come with him; it was her job to scout under the pine trees for any shiny brown glass that hid in the blueberry bushes and rested on the moss. She picked up all the broken ones, the bottles that had been tossed onto the rocks, and put these pieces into a brown paper bag to dispose of safely. Things she avoided: the disintegrating wads of toilet paper; the dark brown Colt butts with white plastic tips; the crumpled pale folds of condoms stuck to the lichen. She dropped whole dusty bottles and any cans she could find into her father's Beer Bag as she found them, careful to lower them by the neck so they just clinked on the others without breaking. They returned these for refund on the drive home. They did this every Sunday. The people at the Beer Store knew Christine by name and she wasn't even legal yet.

Her father had found the note when they had driven out to the lake—it must have fallen out of her jacket pocket when she was in the car. He knew about it all week and didn't tell her. Kevin Lalonde had slipped a note into her locker. Kevin was in Christine's music class, third period. He played clarinet. He and the other clarinets had to suck on their reeds before class, and Kevin Lalonde knew how to flip his upside down with his tongue. The note was folded into a secret-note square. On the inside there was a picture of a chickadee on a branch in front of a red heart. It had come from a girl's notepad, probably from his older sister Judy's. *Come here little chickadee*, he'd written on the paper. He wrote it in pencil, and the word *chickadee* had been misspelled, erased and rewritten, the lines of the original faintly visible underneath. Christine was in her bedroom on Thursday night trying to do her trumpet scales when her father tapped on the door. He asked her to come downstairs with him.

His collection of diseased houseplants lived on a long table in the basement under a purple fluorescent grow-light tube. He collected the plants from the garbage bins behind the garden centre—mildewing African violets, stringy Boston ferns, and pot after plastic pot of pale, drooping spider plants. The purple light was on constantly to stimulate their growth. It made any green they had left in their leaves look muddy and brown. Watering and fertilizing these plants once a week was a chore worth one dollar.

I want to show you something, her father said. He lifted the limp legs of a large spider plant to show her a smaller one underneath. A long white stem connected the new sprouts to the old one. This is a spider plant baby, he said. It comes from here. He pointed to the base of the white stem. If you wanted to start another plant, you could just clip this off, right here. He pinched his fingers to show her. Then you would put that in rich soil and nourish it and let it grow into its own mature plant.

I have to practise my trumpet, Christine said.

Her father cupped the small leaves in the palm of his hand. The best children are like the healthiest plants, he said. They need to be cultivated. And the Bible says, Children are an heritage of the Lord, and the fruit of the womb is his reward. Psalm one-twenty-seven.

Christine's feet felt thick and cold from standing on the concrete floor, like they were made of wet clay. A potato bug groped its way across the plant table. The damp smell of potting soil mouldered in the back of her throat. Her father pulled Kevin's note out of his shirt pocket. He had unfolded the secret square and folded the whole thing in half himself, unevenly. In the dim purple light, the fine lines of the chickadee disappeared, leaving a mottled black stain over a grey heart. I think this belongs to you, he said, and handed it to her. She could barely make out Kevin's writing on the creased paper. The light made his pencil lines almost invisible.

Love is a sacred gift, her father said. He looked at her. Who gave you this?

Nobody, Christine said.

The sexual act is filled with love and grace, Christine. It transcends the sins of petty human selfishness. But only when you are married.

I'm not having sex!

Your sexual purity can be disturbed, even by immoral thoughts.

I am so repulsed right now, said Christine.

Her father smiled at her. The wise father must be dedicated and determined in order to cultivate the sweetest flowers, he said. And you are nothing less than a holy blossom.

He won't let me come see you this weekend, Christine told Sonia on the phone that night. He's going on about God.

No way. He has to let you. Juicy said she'll pay for your ticket.

He says I've been gone too much.

I'll get Juicy to talk to him.

I wish I lived with you.

The suburbs suck, said Sonia. The people of Mississauga are disempowered and inauthentic. I want to move downtown.

When Christine got off the phone, she found her father at the stove skimming congealed fat off a cold pot of chicken-neck broth. The soup was covered with a layer of lumpy yellow wax. A weathered-looking brown bone poked through the surface. He started at the edge, patiently scraping at the yellow gunk little by little, saving each spoonful in a reused yogurt container.

It's a good batch this week, he said. We can make some yellow rice for dinner tomorrow.

I'm going to Mississauga this weekend, Christine said. I'm going.

You love chicken soup and rice, he said.

Juicy is going to call you soon.

He slid the spoon on the edge of the soup pot until it balanced there. He stared into the centre of the pot. Why don't you just stay home this weekend? he asked. We can go out to the lake together.

I told you. I hate going to the stinking lake to pick up other people's dirty beer bottles.

He turned around and looked at her. Christine, he said.

She bent her head so she didn't have to meet his eyes. They pulled at her like those sticky hands you get out of gumball machines.

I wish I knew what made Mississauga so enticing to you, he said.

Well, we don't go into the bush and scavenge other people's garbage, for starters.

I wish you wouldn't think of it that way.

You wish, you wish. I wish you didn't eat dead animals. So.

They stood there across from each other in the kitchen. Her father looked down at his slippered feet on the brown and white kitchen linoleum.

I wish your mother were here, he said. She would know what to say. She would know how to talk to you.

Christine looked at his sad, murky face. There was a shadow in the middle of it, like his nose was sinking into his skull. The hair between his eyebrows looked like the hair on top of a big toe. When he spoke, his teeth were just bones in his mouth.

Get used to it, Christine said. Because she's not ever coming back.

She stomped down the hall and pounded her fist into the door as she slammed it. She stuffed two T-shirts and two pairs of underwear into her backpack. Even through the closed door, she could hear his misery: the spoon tapping against the side of the pot over and over, the sound of steel scraping steel ringing down her spine.

Her aunt Juicy taught music to kindergarteners three days a week. She wore dangly earrings made out of felted wool pompoms. She carried a bright green iPod with *Music is my life!* engraved on the back, and when she was nervous about something, she sang verses from "It's the End of the World as We Know It" as fast as she could. She said it helped her relax. Juicy got pregnant with Sonia when she was nineteen years old, and Sonia's biological father was gay, so they didn't stay together. Bill moved to New Brunswick, where he became a beekeeper and sold herbed oils and vinegars at the Sackville Farmers' Market. Christine has never met him, but she's tasted the wildflower honey.

When Sonia and Juicy picked her up at the bus station on Friday night, the first thing Christine said was, I can't live with my father anymore. I want to move here.

Sonia grabbed Christine's backpack and dropped it in the trunk of the car. Cool, she said. My friend Stoney's brother could get us jobs at the CNE this summer.

Juicy started the car and waited for the girls to get in the back seat and click their seat belts over their chests before she pulled out of the parking lot. Then she asked Christine what was going on.

He stopped going to work, said Christine. And he's smoking in bed.

Gross, said Sonia.

Sonia, be kind, said Juicy.

He wasn't going to let me come here this weekend. He keeps quoting from the Bible.

Uncle Rod's gone done lost the plot, said Sonia.

Oh Christine, Juicy said. I wish you could have known what your father was like when your mother was alive.

I just would have felt sorry for her, Christine said. They were driving on the expressway, passing all the condos with their windows lit up. Christine could see into individual apartments. She could see their fancy light fixtures, dining room tables, blue and green television squares.

Not that it's wrong to be religious, said Juicy. But it is interesting, because Rod didn't even believe in God before your mother died.

Christianity is nothing more than a cult for weak and lonely people, said Sonia. She was applying her lip gloss from a tube with a long white applicator that looked like a Q-tip. The headlights and the traffic made the gloss flash in the dark of the car. Her lips looked silver, then shiny black, then dark red. Poor Uncle Rod, she said, and she twisted the tube of lip gloss shut.

Sonia was sixteen, which was only two years older than Christine. But Sonia had grown up in Toronto and went to an alternative high school downtown and took guitar lessons from a guy who knew the Tragically Hip. Sonia wore Chanel No. 5. She had a huge tester bottle that she swiped from the Bay's fragrance counter. She smoked these little leaves tied up with string that she bought in the bong-and-incense store on Queen Street. Whenever a good band came to town, Sonia used her fake laminated media pass ID and pretended she wrote for Toronto Dot Com. She was good at it. She knew where to find the band after the sound check, what time to wait outside the radio station. Sometimes she talked to the roadies first. But she always got inside the tour bus in the end.

At Juicy's house, Christine borrowed Sonia's terry cloth bathrobe, balled her Greyhound clothes into her backpack, and asked about laundry. There was a smell to her clothes that she could only sense when she got away. It was a residue from her house in Sudbury—a pungent, chalky smell of cigarette smoke, fried onions and damp grief.

Juicy washed Christine's grey hoodie, her *Music is My Boyfriend* and *Metric* T-shirts, her three pairs of blue boycut undies and her jeans in lemon Sunlight powder so she'd smell like a normal human teenager for the weekend. While the clothes were in the dryer, Christine and Sonia sat cross-legged on the white shag carpet in Sonia's bedroom and ate wasabi rice crackers while they planned their tattoos.

I want two sparrows, said Sonia. One here and one here. She tapped her chest just above her B-cup breasts, hitting one with the right hand and one with the left. One for where I've come from, and one for where I'm going.

I want mine to start at my ankle and go all the way up my leg, said Christine. A vine. I'll keep adding to it. Eventually it will wind up around me. She touched the back of her neck. In black, she added.

Black is classic, agreed Sonia.

On Saturday, Juicy drove them into the city. She parked the car in the lot in front of the Harbourfront Centre and said, We'll have dinner on Toronto Island. I'll meet you girls at the ferry in two hours. Sonia wore an olive green shirt-dress and mustard yellow tights with a pair of white-fringed cowboy boots that she found in a store in Parkdale. Christine wore her clean jeans and her hoodie. Juicy let Christine borrow her red Fluevog Mary Janes. They had a short heel in the shape of a heart.

At the Power Plant, there was a room full of resin sculptures that looked like gigantic knuckles and a silent black-and-white film projected on the back wall. Christine stood in front of the screen. A mushroom cloud exploded over a body of water. The plaque said that the images were spliced from over two hundred cameras that recorded nuclear bomb tests near Hawaii after the war. The explosions were mushroom-like. Not just the shape: round on top, with a fat stem. But the stem itself was white and shaggy, just like a forest fungus. Then the cloud grew, and it looked more and more like a cauliflower. Smoke would gather itself up from nothing and then make a firework of cauliflowers.

Sonia got caught stealing a Power Plant notepad from the gift shop, and because of that, they were late meeting Juicy at the ferry terminal and they all had to wait for the next boat. They sat on a bench for an hour and watched a pigeon pick at an old scone sticking out of a paper bag.

I was a little worried at first when you weren't here on time, Juicy told Sonia. Then she hugged Christine around the shoulders. But I knew you were with your cousin, and she'd keep you in line. Right, Christine? You keep Sonia in line.

I want to move here, said Christine. I was serious when I said that.

Juicy twisted the knob of brass hardware on her Roots handbag. We would have to get you into a school, she said.

You could come to my school, said Sonia.

I'll have to talk to your father, Juicy said. Does he know you want this?

Christine stared out at the bushy trees across the water. The ferry was coming back. It looked like it wasn't moving at all, but when she glanced away and then focused on it again, she could see that it was heading towards them. Yes, Christine said. He knows.

The ferry docked at Ward's Island and everyone walked off the boat together. A crowd of people on the island side waited to get on the boat that would bring them back to the city. A white-haired man in the lineup winked at Christine when she passed him. He had a wide-brimmed hat and rested his weight on a purple metallic stick that looked like a ski pole. A wooden bead cinched the strings of his hat together under his neck.

It was so quiet on the island with the city skyline crouched on the other side of the harbour. Juicy took the long way, leading them through the trees. The green-grey sliver of a tiny garter snake wriggled through the leaves right in front of Christine's shoes and disappeared into the scrubby bushes. The crunchy whine of red-winged blackbirds buzzed in the trees. Christine's ears were ringing. A flash of brown glass and a blue label in the dogwood branches. Probably Labatt's.

It's so beautiful here, sighed Juicy.

I partied here once, said Sonia. Geoffrey Duguay's mother's boyfriend used to live here. We had a bonfire, it was potent.

When was that? asked Juicy.

Sonia looked at Christine and rolled her eyes. Never mind, she said.

They ate dinner outside, on the patio at the café near the boardwalk. Juicy ordered a glass of white wine for herself and sparkling elderflowers for the girls. They each had the same thing, because it was the only vegetarian dish on the menu: pasta salad with white beans, spring peas and watercress. For dessert, flourless chocolate cake. The sunlight fell through the leaves, making spots of shade on their faces.

Isn't this just blissful? asked Juicy. Isn't it like we're eating dinner in the middle of an enchanted forest?

We heard wolves howling the night of the party, said Sonia.

There aren't any wolves here, said Juicy.

How do you know that? said Sonia.

Families live here. It's not a real forest, there aren't any wolves.

Maybe they were just dogs pretending, said Christine.

Late Saturday night, after they went to bed, Sonia lined up five shot glasses in a row, filled them with Goldschläger, and told Christine she wasn't going to let her go to sleep until she drank every one of them. It was always hard to leave Sonia. On Sunday afternoon, at the bus station, Sonia gave Christine a mixed CD without a case. She pulled a Sharpie out of her jacket and wrote directly on the disc: *Christine Christine Christine*. The words formed a circle. Everything made her dizzy.

Don't listen to this till the bus leaves, she said.

Christine pressed the CD into her Discman. Her father wouldn't let her have an iPod because he said she was too young for technology that expensive. He was a relic from another age.

Suck on these peppermints, Sonia told her. They'll help your stomach.

Juicy hugged her tight around the waist and Christine felt a lump in her throat.

He won't let me—he won't—Christine said.

I'll do what I can, Juicy said.

Christine handed Sonia a folded note. Don't open this till the bus is gone, she said. The note said: *YOU BETTER COME TO THE BIG NICKEL ASAP!*

Thanks babe, Sonia said, and held the note between two fingers like a cigarette.

On the bus, Christine tucked herself in with her knees crunched up against the seat ahead of her. The bus upholstery was the colour of a brown bread sandwich. She had both seats to herself until the last person got on the bus. He had blond hair that fanned out from his head like it had been charged with static at Science North. Black jeans and a leather jacket, tight at the waist and zipped up halfway. He leaned over to push a red nylon duffle bag into the overhead shelf above Christine. He rocked his pelvis as the bag fit into place, which was somehow both repulsive and alluring.

He sat down next to her, leaned back and exhaled. He was skinny, but his weight was enough to make the seat creak. There was a smokiness about him, Vantage menthols and creosote-soaked railroad ties, that reminded Christine of her father.

From Toronto to Parry Sound, he sat beside her without saying a word. Christine edged her elbow away from the armrest between them and held her hands in her lap. She listened to Sonia's CD on her Discman: a mix of the Ramones, the Doors and the Who. The pine trees outside flew by the window all in rows. Christine focused on the spaces between the trees as they passed. She watched for moose until it got too dark to see anything at all. The man must have fallen asleep beside her; he hadn't moved for three hours.

The bus stopped at the McDonald's in Parry Sound. They pulled into the parking lot and the driver said, Fifteen minutes. If you need a smoke, please do so outside the coach. The bus made a hissing sound and the door opened like it was gasping for air. Christine wanted to get something to eat, but the man was still asleep right next to her. The other passengers started to stretch and stand. They moved stiffly, like newly hatched reptiles.

Excuse me, Christine said.

The man opened his eyes and turned and looked right at her. His irises were the yellow of canned pineapple. The pull of his jacket made the stretched sound of twisting balloons.

Let's go get a hot apple pie, he said, like they were old friends.

I want a cherry one, Christine told him.

We'll get you a hot cherry pie, then. Come on.

He bought the cherry pie for her even though she offered to pay for it herself. The cashier folded the top of the paper bag twice, flashing bright pink fake nails. Christine reached for the bag on the counter and her eyes met the cashier's, so she smiled and said thank you and walked out. She could feel the man following her. She got on the bus and led the way to their seats. They ate together as the bus pulled out of the parking lot. Christine blew on the cherries before each bite to cool them off.

When they were finished, he said, That hit the spot, didn't it? His Adam's apple quivered under bristly skin when he spoke. He hardly had lips at all. And yet, even though he was ugly, there was something sexy about him.

Yeah, Christine said. Thanks.

I just love the apple, he said. But you think the cherry's better, don't you?

Christine looked at him. I like apple too, she said.

What I mean is, I'm interested in your opinion. The tastes of young women—especially the Northern type. See, I'm opening a restaurant myself.

Really, Christine said. She remembered Sonia's peppermints in her pocket, felt for one, and popped it in her mouth. Sweet mint cut through sweet cherry.

In Thunder Bay, he said. A bagel place. And it's all about the market research, I'll tell you.

You going to sell apple pies? she asked.

Well, no, I'm going to be selling bagels. But—he paused and watched Christine transfer the peppermint to her other cheek with her tongue—but I was thinking that I could sell cherry-flavoured bagels. What do you think of that?

Christine rolled the candy back across her tongue, making a wet knocking sound on her teeth. She curled her lips into a little pocket. I think it's disgusting, she said.

It wasn't until they were an hour outside of Sudbury that he asked for her name. The inside of the bus was dark, with scattered beams of light aimed at opened magazines and paperbacks on passengers' laps. The smell of greasy burger wrappers lingered in the air.

I'm Sonia, Christine said.

Pleased to know you, Sonia, said Bruce Corbiere.

They kissed for almost an hour. Her lips were wet and rubbery, but her limbs were all fuses and wires. Outside, the lights looked sharp and clear. She considered staying on the bus.

How old are you? Bruce asked.

How old do you think I am?

He looked at her. Seventeen?

A warm pulse in her chest from this: he thought she was even older than Sonia.

When she didn't respond, he looked uneasy.

Sixteen?

She grinned. Don't worry, she said. It's not like I'm going to call my mommy or anything. She pushed back her sleeve, looked at her bare wrist. What time is it? she asked him.

It is the time for us to part, he said. Farewell, Sweet Sonia.

Good luck with your bagels, Christine said. She wrestled with her backpack, trying to find what was catching the strap.

Wait, he said. Let me help. With one move, he released the strap from the footrest. Then he said, Sonia. I'm going to need your phone number. For more market research.

Christine wrote it on the palm of his hand with a black felt-tip marker, and as she pressed the ink into his skin, she made a silent wish: Please make something happen. It was a wimpy, ambiguous wish and she didn't even know what it meant. The bus pulled into the station. Her father would be outside, waiting for her. She held Bruce Corbiere's hand where she'd written her phone number. She pushed his fingers until they curled inward and made a fist.

Call in the evening, she told him. Okay? Like after five.

You have someone picking you up? he asked her.

Yeah, Christine said. She didn't say: My father.

Well, you take care of yourself, then. It was a pleasure.

She thought he might try to kiss her again. But he didn't. He just waved goodbye to her with one hand, and he kept her phone number closed in his fist.

When Christine was standing in the aisle with everyone waiting to get off the bus, she noticed a tall woman wearing a white woven scarf. The woman stepped off the bus and scanned the cars outside the station. Christine followed, watching her. The woman bent down next to the belly of the bus and picked up an old red suitcase with a crinkled paper tag hanging from the handle. The mangled voice on the loudspeaker called out: For passengers travelling to Thunder Bay, your coach is located on platform three, preparing to depart.

The woman in the scarf bit her lip in a worried way. She was looking for someone. Then she found him. He was wearing a green and black plaid jacket with leather patches on the elbows. He appeared to rise out of a big wood-panelled station wagon. The man took the red suitcase out of her hand and said something to her. She laughed. They kissed each other. They looked strange and out of date, like they had just rolled out of a vintage shop in Kensington Market.

There was no sign of Christine's father's pickup truck.

Years later, when Christine tells this story, she'll say that she waited for her father for half an hour before she started to worry. When she watched the bus leave the lot, on its way north to Thunder Bay, Bruce Corbiere looked out the window at her and pressed his fingertips against the window to say goodbye. She felt in her jacket pocket for her Discman and couldn't find it, realized she'd forgotten it on the Greyhound, and then wondered if Bruce Corbiere had stolen it. She'll say that after all of the other people had been picked up and driven away in cars and taxis, when she was left alone in the station with the blips of the arcade game flashing in the empty room behind her, when she felt in her pocket for quarters and headed to the pay phone to call her father, before she dialed and listened to the phone ring and ring and ring at the other end, before she called a taxi to come and get her, before she put her key into the lock and stepped into her dark house, turned on the hall light and saw the folded piece of paper on the table, before she read her father's last note, before calling Juicy and telling her what happened and then lying down in front of the television just to listen to the people talking while she waited four hours for her aunt to drive all the way up to Sudbury in the middle of the night, before the funeral and the packing of boxes and moving down to live with Sonia, just like she wanted—before any of that happened, Christine will say that she'd seen the ghosts of her parents at the bus station that night, but that she just didn't recognize them at first, because they looked so young and happy.

Prognosis

Dear Mrs. B——,

Twenty years have passed since we have spoken. I know you haven't always agreed with our lifestyle, but I was surprised when your letters stopped entirely. It's been almost a decade. Your unwillingness to argue about our life decisions in recent years led me to believe that you were either resting comfortably in a divot of calcified judgment or that you had finally made peace with our choices. I had hoped it was the latter, but I just discovered that your silence was more menacing than I had feared. Your resentment is palpable and extraordinary, and it has tested the architecture of my marriage. I don't know what has been more distressing—having to justify our *modus vivendi* every time I was in contact with you, sensing your disapproval from a distance during these years of silence, or learning that you have actually been in contact with my husband all this time.

Gabe has told me about your diagnosis. He said that you might not even live to see next summer. You know that I have little faith in the trappings of organized religions, so I will not say that I am praying for you. Instead, I will say that you are in my thoughts, and that I am writing you this letter because I have also been silent for too long.

I wish you had given this place another chance, come for a second visit. We were so young back then—just married, barely making enough money to pay for the wood we needed to build this house. We were inexperienced landowners and we weren't ready for you. I'm sorry you had such a hard time of it, especially your nausea from the boat and your constant chill (even when the wood stove was raging with fire, you managed to find corners and pockets of cold in our house). Our outdoor shower frightened you even more than the dark forest behind the property. But I never thought that you would take these things personally—as though we had created an unlivable environment so you would never come back.

Many things have changed since your visit so long ago. We've had solar panels installed, and even though we've kept the outhouse, we've landscaped the path to it, and the walls are insulated—it's all much more substantial than when you were here. But you probably know these things already, don't you?

Here is something you might not know.

I have always been slightly afraid of you. I know that you looked at Gabe as your finest creative success, that you had the highest expectations for his future. But I could never be sure what you thought of me. I could read disapproval everywhere: in your gestures, your vocal intonations, in the very syntax in your letters. Although I sensed that you always wished for a more studious wife for your son—someone who managed to finish her doctorate, at least—I shouldn't have built that feeling into a stone citadel.

Instead of putting energy into our broken relationship over these years, I've been studying your work and writing. Your extensive research on the relationship between faith and reason is very compelling. I've read your work on the epistemological diversity of current Catholic theologists and your essays on rationalism and anti-rationalism and how it affects political and cultural oppression within Catholic universities. Your knowledge is substantial and intimidating. I was especially intrigued by your latest book, *I See Holy: Religious Simulacra and Pareidolia*. It relates to an issue that has perplexed me for most of my life.

As I sat alone on the porch this morning, apprehensive and hurt by the news of these years of secret letters and phone calls, I wondered why I had never asked you about this issue before now. I studied the shoreline and contemplated the creatures hidden under the sand. I questioned my own motivations for making a home on this island. I calculated the degree of damage done to my relationship, a marriage built on honesty and trust.

Do you remember, the last time we spoke, I told you that I had a condition, a malfunctioning tear duct from a childhood surgery? I asked Gabe to explain it to you, and he did—but he was telling you about a medical condition that I don't actually have. The real story is stranger than that. What I told you was an excuse for something I could not understand myself. I realize now that you would likely have been comfortable discussing it quite openly—in your work, after all, you spend a great deal of time assembling conceptual parentheses to contain matters of an abstract or philosophical nature. What held me back then was fear (again, fear!)—not entirely of your disregard, though I believed this to be the case. It was my own fear of the inexplicable.

When I was six years old, my mother saw a vision of the Virgin Mary in an Ida Red apple in the produce section of Food City. As you know, it's become a bit of a cliché now—last year a vision of Mary in a grilled cheese sandwich sold for $28,000 in an auction, and the image of Jesus Christ in a water stain brought hundreds of people to a concrete wall in a Chicago underpass. In your paper *Apparitions of God: Divine Intervention or Delusion?* you write about the face of God spotted in the smoke of the Twin Towers. But this apple appeared to my mother years ago, when we were still surprised by the one or two satellites we'd catch moving across the night sky; before there were cellphones and BlackBerrys; before farmers began to introduce DNA from Arctic char into our tomatoes. Had it happened today, my mother might have put the apple up for auction on eBay.

My mother dabbled briefly in the United Church when she was a child, but she was never what I would call a religious woman (though you should know that she has always said good things about you. She has never forgotten the lilac suit you wore to our wedding. Was it a European design? My mother searched for a reasonable duplicate for many years). I was not baptized. At the age of six, I'm not even sure I could have identified the figure of Mary anywhere, other than in a lit-up manger in our neighbour's front yard every December—a glowing blue-cloaked figure kneeling by a plastic baby that appeared to be strapped to a toboggan.

On the day that it happened, my mother pushed the clattering steel grocery cart up to the apple bin and stopped there, moving her hands together in front of her chest like a knot she was trying to untangle. People looked at her. She ignored them, muttering, staring straight ahead at the pile of apples. She ignored me. In a rare demonstration of adventurousness (I was a placid child, not given to roaming), I left my mother and wandered on my own until I found the bulk food section. I settled myself in front of the bottom shelf and set to unwrapping sticky glittermints and chewing on fingerfuls of rubbery licorice nibs until a skinny red-coated stock boy pulled me off the floor and back to the front of the store to find out whom I belonged to. There stood my mother, a holy look on her face and a plastic bag full of apples in one fist. She held the "special" apple in her other hand. When she saw me, she bent down and put the fruit to my face. *Look*, she said.

Now, my mother had been in the care of a psychiatrist for most of that year, sometimes away in "retreat" for weeks at a time. I wasn't told these details until I was much older, and I don't know what frightened me more: her absence, or seeing her anxious and unwell. I was late for school one morning because she wouldn't let me out of the house before she had sewn a careful lining of tinfoil to the inside of my winter toque. She cancelled our subscription to the newspaper because she read mysterious, malevolent messages there. She watched television with a notepad in hand, scribbling down pieces of dialogue. My mother's fear was palpable; it was an electric, metallic charge in the atmosphere. When I was six years old, my mother was my closest friend. I was afraid of her agitation, yet I hated to be away from her. It was not an easy time.

It feels important to note that the day in the grocery store, when my mother found the apple, she was not buzzing with anxiety. She was gentle and clear. I was not afraid of her. This all happened a long time ago, but I remember that for certain.

Five years later, a peculiar thing happened to me. One afternoon, curled in an easy chair reading *Harriet the Spy*, I discovered that if I pulled on my left earlobe, water would come out from behind my ear. The water was warmish and there wasn't very much of it, but it startled me, and I made a sound that brought my mother into the living room. She asked me, *What happened?* And I had to tell her: I pulled my ear and water came out.

My mother had been in a stable period for at least two years. Calmly, she inspected my ear. She rubbed and poked the spot I located for her. And even though there was no hole, crack or puncture in my skin, the water came out for her too: a trickle that I could feel like a teardrop sliding down my neck.

My mother had never mentioned the legendary apple after that day in the grocery store. I suspect that she told my father and he had credited it to her paranoia. My memories from these years are vague and scattered now, but I do not recall my mother modifying her behaviour in any way that would signify having experienced a "miracle." She did not begin attending Mass, she did not speak to me about the importance of prayer, and as far as I knew, she did not acquire even one religious icon—not even a rosary. Despite this, when my ear produced water that day, it somehow became clear to my mother that this was a direct result of my witnessing a miracle in the Food City as a child, and she said so. She said, *I can't explain it, but we should celebrate.*

That afternoon, she took me for a manicure and pedicure at an upscale salon, and a very nice lunch in a restaurant with a waterfall in the courtyard. I had a drink made with layers of cranberry and grapefruit juice, and my mother had a glass of white wine. We toasted the Virgin together, admiring our newly polished nails.

I began to explore Catholicism on my own, with a customary preteen focus on the unexplainable, the paranormal and the macabre—or, as these things are called in the Church, miracles. My mother certainly did not encourage my investigation. I imagine my father was aware of my obsession with stories about weeping statues and historical Marian sightings (from the Miracle Tortilla in

New Mexico to those four little girls in Spain who could run up mountains, their feet moving without touching the ground) and my fascination with famous cases of stigmata, but he did not interfere, even when I decided that I wanted to start going to church. My mother hated the idea. I was nearing the age when girls begin to abhor their mothers. If I had been older, I'd like to think that I would have been more sympathetic to my mother's misgivings.

My mother agreed to drive me to Our Lady of Perpetual Help every Sunday. She would only allow me to go if she accompanied me. I didn't know the source of her reluctance—I assumed that it was based on her old paranoia, but she later admitted that she was trying to protect her impressionable daughter from such a dogmatic faith. Regardless, the routine didn't last more than five or six weeks. The services were long and tedious, and I was disappointed to discover that, despite the name of the parish I had chosen for myself, there was never any exploration of Marian visitations or miraculous visions during Mass.

I met Beverly Nauffsinger on my last "trial" Sunday at Our Lady of Perpetual Help. I remember Beverly as an older woman, but now I wonder if she was even forty. She wore several thin gold chains and petite crucifixes in a tangle around her neck. As she spoke, she fiddled with the complicated knots, her fingers moving over the gold crosses and miniature Christ figures consistently and ineffectually, as though she were fingering a rosary. Beverly had travelled to the United States to hear the Virgin Mary speak through a woman named Mrs. Francis Butler (this is the same Francis Butler you wrote about in your essay *Solar Apparitions and Marian Visitations in the Southern United States*). Beverly went to the Butlers' 150-acre hunting farm in Quality, Kentucky, and she said the scent of roses filled the air and the sun pulsated before her eyes and divided into multiple lights. She said she could look straight at the sun and that the Lord protected her eyes, and that since then, she was able to see colours that she was not able to see before. Beverly showed me a rosary that she purchased in Quality. The beads were little coloured bits of carved wood—blue, green, yellow and red—connected with twists of gold wire. *When I bought this rosary*, Beverly whispered to me, *these wires were one hundred percent pure silver*. She pointed to a piece of wire with one purple-painted fingernail. *Now they're pure gold.* She crossed herself. *That's a miracle, right there*, she said. Later, my mother told me that it was widely known in our community that, while she was inarguably a kind-hearted person, Beverly Nauffsinger was delusional.

Years passed, and so did my religious phase. My mother battled with anxiety and occasional bouts of depression, but nothing took her completely out of this reality. Occasionally, my father would tug at my earlobe in a teasing way, saying, *Any holy water in there today?* I was an awkward teenager, and my relationship with my father had devolved into nothing more than self-conscious attempts at light conversation—the earlobe joke one of our only reliable physical interactions. (Perhaps it is different when raising sons. Does a mother remain close to her son, without awkwardness, even through puberty?) I did not experience the watery ear phenomenon again, even though I had spent long nights tugging and pressing my left ear as I tried to fall asleep, while reading or watching television, and, of course, those Sundays while attending Mass. The water, quite simply, had vanished.

That is, until I met your son. After graduating high school, I accepted an offer from the London School of Economics and began my studies in cultural anthropology. I rarely visited home, using my holidays for travel and research. I met Gabe in Spain, as you know; I was in San Sebastián presenting a paper at a conference on Philosophy, Democracy and Medicine. There were more than two hundred people in that amphitheatre, but when I saw Gabe sitting in the third row, the room contracted, and I knew that I had already known him for the rest of my life. On the night of our first kiss, when he slipped his palm against my cheek and the nape of my neck, it happened. A bewildered look passed over his face. I could feel the water trickling down, but before I could say, *Don't worry, it's not what you think* (what exactly I meant by that, I wonder now), he kissed me anyway, and the water pooled into my clavicle, furtive and sleek.

Gabe never had a chance to meet my father. My parents had gone on a cruise through the Spanish Virgin Islands for their fortieth wedding anniversary. On his second night on the ship, my father suffered a massive stroke. He did not live through the night; my mother and my father's body were flown home on a direct flight from

Puerto Rico. My mother had an acute anxiety attack and a subsequent nervous breakdown that had her hospitalized for several weeks. Soon after presenting my paper, I took a leave from my graduate work and returned to Canada to be with her.

How did Gabe explain all of this to you? Did he ever tell you that he left France because of me? Or did he tell you that the University of British Columbia presented a counter-offer that he couldn't refuse? Would you have blamed me, if you had known the truth?

In the years that we dated, as he worked his way through medical school, Gabe was fascinated by my condition. He investigated it tirelessly. I do not, in fact, have a malfunctioning tear duct, though there are those who do; my symptoms match theirs, which is why I adopted that explanation so readily. The truth is that there is, so far, no answer to my little mystery.

Mrs. B——, I wish you could have met my mother before my father's death. She used to be a vibrant woman, full of sharp witticisms. I know she would have had many thoughts on your research and critical work. My mother is my only family—I have no siblings (neither does she) and I have never really known my father's family (they live in Missouri). After a year of careful therapeutic care, my mother was again stable, present and lucid. On my thirtieth birthday, during an extended visit from my mother (she made herself at home on our island that summer, sleeping on a foam mattress on our back deck, navigating her way through the woods with a compass, learning to cultivate wild mushrooms and make jam from salal berries—there is such a contrast between her experience of this place and your own), we found ourselves sitting on the back deck, sipping our signature drinks, cranberry and grapefruit. She asked me, mentioning the apple for the first time in nineteen years, *Do you believe that I saw her that day?*—and my ear instantly began to drip in response. Yes, I said, of course I believe you saw her. She closed her eyes and smiled, and at that moment I felt closer to my mother than ever before. We both cried with relief. The water from my ear dripped along with my tears; I had to excuse myself to pat myself dry.

The reason I write you this now is that it has been fifteen years since then, and only once has the water from my ear returned. Last week, Gabe came in from the car, walking with a peculiar quietness, his footfalls soft and deliberate in the hallway. His eyes were red, and I guessed that he'd been crying. Then Gabe told me that he had just talked to you on the phone. He told me, finally, that he'd been communicating with you all of these years—behind my back, at your insistence, writing letters and mailing them secretly, accepting phone calls from a private cell number and emailing you from his personal address. I felt the edges of our marriage disintegrating. The volatile cliffs of secrecy and regret hanging over us, immense, lifelong, volcanic. His breath was like a rash against my skin. But he also told me your prognosis, Mrs. B——. And it was then that I felt the trickle along my neck.

We tried to speak to each other honestly. We tried to discuss the details of his flight, and how long he would be away, and what the absence would mean for the projects we are working on together. We talked a little about what would happen if I wasn't here when he came home. And the water continued to leak. It dribbled down my throat and my T-shirt caught the liquid, a circle of wet cotton. It continued to flow even when Gabe pressed his hand to the crease behind my ear, the softest place on my skull, to find its origin. His hand filled with water. There was nothing that we could do to stop it. It was two hours before it ceased. And in those two hours, we finally heard each other.

I am telling you all of this now, perhaps selfishly, almost certainly too late, but in an attempt to give you the most significant thing about myself that I can gather: this mystery. I hope that this will make more sense to you than it ever did to me.

Respectfully,
Magda

Paul Farenbacher's Yard Sale

Paul Farenbacher always told me, Never call yourself a salesperson. What you do isn't *sales*, he'd say. You aren't in *sales*. What you are doing is providing people with an opportunity. This is what you do. Sometimes. It's not even what you *do*. It's not who you are. You are Meredith; you are a lovely woman. And Meredith reads and enjoys the theatre and spending time outdoors. Meredith also sometimes provides an opportunity for an individual to purchase excellent cleaning products. See? This is not sales. Never say you are a salesperson.

Paul Farenbacher provided opportunities for individuals to purchase products for twenty-five years before he retired, before he got sick. He started out selling detergents and disinfectants—not too different from what I do now, in fact—but after that, he sold cookware: heavy, enamel-coated cast iron. He also had a brief stint selling vitamins and nutritional supplements made from Blu-Green algae. I still have a questionable canister of this powdered seaweed at home. He claimed it strengthened his immune system. I have used it exactly once. I blended it into a Blu-Green Banana Smoothie, as suggested on the side panel. The powder turned the liquefied fruit such a disturbing shade of turquoise that I was moved to pour the lumpy miracle cure down the toilet. I snapped the plastic lid onto the tin and tucked it into the back of my cupboard. I should throw it away, but I can't.

I would really like a cup of coffee. It's nine o'clock on Saturday morning and I'm standing on the Farenbachers' front lawn with their son, Trevor. I'm trying to make eye contact with the early birds as they swarm the rack of Paul Farenbacher's suits, looking for bargains. A money belt loaded with coins hugs my waist and I am grateful for the anchor. It's beautiful today—drifts of petals from the cherry trees have sifted into small piles on both sides of the curb. A light breeze and the petals stir like confetti in a snow globe. Trevor is having a hard time with this sale. He's going around behind his mother's back with a black Sharpie, marking the prices up when she's not looking. He came back from Costa Rica this winter, when his father got sick. He said he wanted to restructure his business and get certified to teach kitesurfing here in Victoria. I wonder what he wants to do now.

Paul Farenbacher used to live in Costa Rica. One of the ten windiest places in the world, he told me. That's why Trevor was there. But in the sixties, Paul Farenbacher was involved in something called the Instinctive Nutrition Movement, a group who smelled their food and then decided to eat it based on their intuitive reaction to the odour. They used to eat live shellfish, he told me. Right out of the ocean. Something about the briny tang was intuitively comforting to the ancient reptilian mind—it triggered memories, perhaps, of an amoebic past spent suspended in saline—so they would gnaw at live prawns and crabs still blue from the waves, bite into the salty bodies before boiling water could taint them.

I've never been to Costa Rica. I've never been east of Osoyoos, British Columbia.

Trevor's mother, Margaret, stands in the middle of the lawn, next to Paul Farenbacher's reclining chair. One of the early birds approaches her. The woman is wearing a pale blue trench coat. She has very curly hair. It's scraped off her face and cinched in a tight puff at the base of her head. The woman looks at Margaret, she looks at the chair, and she bites her lip, thinking.

Can I sit in it? she asks.

Of course, says Margaret. Use the lever, get a feel for it.

Just pretend you're in your living room, Bruce says. Try to ignore us.

If only it were that easy, says Trevor.

Bruce is Margaret's new boyfriend. Today is only the second time I've seen them together. The first time was the wet and uncomfortable Thursday evening at Welsh & Bloom Funeral Home, only two months ago, when the whole neighbourhood came out on the rainiest night of the winter to see Paul Farenbacher arranged in a box in a jaunty pinstripe suit I'd never seen him wear before (such wide, bold stripes: he looked as though he were dressed for a performance in Vegas). A collection of Paul's old cronies was there, from all his years of work—the cookware men, the detergent and spray disinfectant men, the Blu-Green algae men (who were actually mostly women)—huddled under the dripping canvas awning out front, a cluster of khaki overcoats under a cloud of smoke that condensed into fog. The sixty-year-old's version of extreme sport: smoking at a funeral sponsored by lung cancer. The risk! The bravado! And Margaret Farenbacher in the front row, tucked into a pearl-grey suit like an altocumulus formation, managing to look parched in the rainstorm, her face powdered, her lipstick bleeding into cracks, her hair shellacked into feathers. Beside her, the tall man in black we all now know as Bruce, or *Margaret's new boyfriend*, looking like he could use a cigarette himself.

Margaret has sold the Farenbacher bungalow and is moving in with Bruce, which is the reason for this yard sale. Perhaps that's why Margaret chose to dress her husband in pinstripes on the day he was buried; in a muted way, she was also celebrating her engagement to Bruce. I don't mean to sound unkind. I've lived next door to the Farenbachers for thirty years. I grew up with Trevor. I learned how to ride a bicycle in their driveway. Paul and

Margaret used to babysit me. Margaret can be a very lovely woman.

I still live with my parents, in the house where I grew up. I run a small business called Scrub Goddess, a line of all-natural household cleansers. I started by mixing baking soda, a mild abrasive, with clove oil. I made batches of the stuff in the kitchen sink. I called it Artemis Powder and stuck a pink label on the jar—the same kind of jar you'd find filled with Parmesan cheese at the grocery store—and started selling it door to door. Business has grown, and I've converted our unfinished basement into a workable industrial unit. My mother helps me run my booth at the trade shows. Ten years ago, if someone had told me this would be my life, I would never have believed it.

It's comfortable, the woman says, after she's sat in the chair, pressed her lower back against the lumbar pillow, experimented with the lever, and hauled herself out again. It looks very new.

Oh, it is, says Margaret. It's hardly been used.

You're unbelievable, says Trevor.

She just means that it's in excellent condition, I say to Trevor.

The woman asks Margaret, Why are you selling it?

Bruce nestles Margaret's shoulders under his big arm. Well, he says, I already have a leather club chair, and there's just not enough room for the sectional, the loveseat *and* two big chairs in my living room.

Margaret pats the back of the La-Z-Boy like it's a dog. It's been very good to us, she says, but it's time to let it go to a new home now.

I'll need a hand if I get it, the woman says. Let me think. She starts to walk away.

Don't think about it too long! calls Bruce.

Margaret is wearing a pungent perfume. The thick scent hangs around her like a sticky brown cloud. She has styled her grey hair so that it wafts up off her head like layers of meringue. She wears caramel-coloured loafers that sink into the grass. They're dark around the toes, stained from the dew.

She'll come back, says Bruce. Don't worry.

Do I look worried? Trevor says.

Trev, says Margaret.

Trevor turns away from her, walks over to the boxes set in the shady grass in the front of the yard. I follow him. Do you want to take a break? I ask. He ignores me.

He crouches by the milk crate, his back arched in a C-curve, and silently flips through his father's old record albums. He looks like his father—smaller than average, even a bit shorter than I am. Stocky, with the kind of muscles that I've always thought were good for rock climbing or skateboarding. We kissed once. In the kitchen at the Murphys' annual holiday block party. Trevor came in looking to refill his glass with something, and there I was, refilling my own. We were both drunk. He pressed me up against the refrigerator when we kissed, and my back slid over a button on the fridge door that made a pile of ice cubes fall out. They spilled all over the floor like a cold, glittering win at a private slot machine.

When I found out that Paul Farenbacher was sick, I started to come over to visit during the day, when Margaret was at the office. Trevor was still in Costa Rica. I made miso broth with thin slices of green onion and I served it to him in a deep red and white soup bowl I found in Chinatown. We listened to the radio together. I offered to make him a Blu-Green Banana Smoothie once, and he made a face and smacked the air with his hand. Those people don't know shit from putty, he said. Throw that stuff away. The smell of Windex made him feel sick, so I spritzed their windows and countertops with my spearmint-scented Demeter Spray.

He bought the La-Z-Boy as a gift for himself soon after his diagnosis. He said he'd spent his whole life fighting it, but that it was finally time to recognize the desires of his inner lazy man. He showed me a catalogue of chairs for lazy people: slots for the remote controls, coolers in the armrests, space for a whole six-pack of beer. Paul ordered the basic model in solid blue. After the chemotherapy, this was the only place he could still feel comfortable. He often spent the night there, in the reclined position, a blanket tucked up around his chin. He'd lost all of his thick white hair—he'd gone silver in his twenties, and as long as I'd known him, his hair was a source of pride—but he refused to wear a toque over his bald head, even on cool nights. My head is not a teapot, he'd say.

Trevor finally says something to me. Should I keep this? he asks. He's holding an Arlo Guthrie album.

You keep whatever you think, I say. Keep it, if you want it.

He slips it back into the milk crate and stands up. No. I have enough.

Why don't we get some coffee. Get out of here for a while.

I'll take the whole crate, says a man behind us. I turn around. A pair of sunglasses hang around his neck on a thick orange plastic cord. He already has his wallet out in his hands. His fingers press two green bills out of the crease. He says, I'll give you forty bucks and I'll take the record player and this whole crate of albums off your hands.

The record player alone is twenty-five, says Trevor.

I'll give you forty for the whole shebang.

What did I just say? says Trevor.

I put my hand on Trevor's back and feel his spine through the cotton. That's fine, I say gently. We can do forty. Do you need a hand getting it to your car?

The man is still looking at Trevor. No, thank you, he says carefully. I've got it.

After he's gone, Trevor says, Well, he just cleaned up, didn't he.

It's just five dollars. It doesn't matter.

Whatever, he says. I hardly remember Dad using that record player anyway.

Your dad liked his music, though, I say.

What do you mean by that? Trevor looks at me.

What I meant was that Paul Farenbacher liked *his* music, the records that just drove off in a blue car with a yellow "Save Our Troops" decal. He had no use for contemporary artists. I'd burned him CDs thinking I could find something with a classic roots feel, a new collaboration he'd like despite himself: Billy Bragg playing with Wilco, Robert Plant with Alison Krauss. He thanked me for the albums but never listened to them more than once. Eventually I accepted that he simply preferred the sound of his own records.

Your father had strong opinions, I say to Trevor. I mean, he knew what he liked and didn't like. I used to listen to Emmylou Harris with him, I say.

Trevor looks at me slantwise. How is your father doing, Meredith? He must like his new job, sitting on the couch testing candy all day.

He's actually on the computer all day.

I was only kidding.

My father used to work at the Island Dairy plant before he injured himself. He had an accident while sweeping the floor with a cheap broom—the plastic handle fell off mid-sweep, and the metal rod, which was sharp and jagged at the end under the plastic cap, slipped and punctured his forearm, just past his wrist, severing a tendon and leaving him with numbness in three of the four fingers of his right hand. He's since gone on disability, which has significantly cut the household income even though he was only a few years away from retirement anyway, and now he stays at home and helps my mother track promotions for her Candy-of-the-Month mail order business. We're all self-made people out here on Linden Street.

He's doing better, I tell Trevor. He's starting to write with his left hand. It's almost as good as his right. You can only tell on some letters, because he writes them backwards.

What letters does he write backwards?

I think about it. S, I say. And N.

Trevor pulls out a ratchet set. Mom, are you sure you want to get rid of this? he says. You can use these, you know. These are good tools.

I don't even know what that's called, says Margaret. I wouldn't know how to use it. I have my hammer and my screwdriver set and my little power drill, and I'm just fine with that.

I have a ratchet set, says Bruce.

I'm sure you do, says Trevor.

I'm going to make a coffee run, I say. Who wants coffee?

Oh, Meredith, I'd just love one, says Margaret. Cream and sugar, please.

Thanks for helping us out, Meredith, says Bruce. We sure do appreciate you being here today. He adds: Milk, no sugar for me.

Bruce is tall, and he stands with his chest raised. He's in excellent shape for a man well into his sixties. His frame is classic strength. He has large hands that have seen some physical work, hands you feel you can trust. Bruce is not a heartless man. He has a good face. I don't blame Margaret for wanting to move in with him.

Margaret says, Before I forget, Meredith, I'm almost out of my Artemis Powder.

I might have a jar kicking around for you, I tell her.

How's that going? asks Trevor.

Business is good, I tell him. People don't want to use chemicals anymore. Everyone is afraid of cancer. Then I stop, realizing what I just said.

Sorry.

Don't be.

I didn't mean that—

It's okay.

Margaret has wandered over to the card table that's set up on the other side of the yard. She rearranges piles of mismatched dishware, putting the large plates on the bottom, saucers and bowls on top. I watch her turn some of these pieces upside down over the lawn, dumping out the cherry blossoms that have collected inside. She looks at the mugs, and one by one shakes the petals out of those too. Then she straightens all of the mugs so that their handles are pointing in the same direction.

Sorry if I'm being a bastard today, Trevor says to me.

You aren't really. It's okay.

It's because when I listen to myself talk, the words sound ridiculous.

I know, I tell him. I feel the same way.

I'm just aggravated. Don't listen to me today.

A woman with a vinyl clutch purse is moving through the rack of clothes with her fingers like she's leafing through office files. Then she turns around and leaves the yard, her purse tucked under her arm. Trevor says, When we're talking, it's so obvious that we're alive.

We could be quiet, I say.

No, he says. That's awkward.

He's playing with his T-shirt. Rolling the edge of the fabric between his thumb and forefinger so it makes a tight tube. Then letting it go so it hangs in a curl at his waist. I want to reach out and press the curl down and feel his hip under my hand.

I miss your dad, I say. I spent a lot of time with him this winter.

I know, he says.

Paul Farenbacher's briefcase is on the grass by my feet. I have a collection of old battered suitcases I've picked up from antique shops and estate sales. I love them. They're all in my living room, holding my tax returns and receipts from the past seven years. I have to keep the paperwork for that long in case I'm audited; every year someone starts a rumour that they're digging for fraud associated with natural health trends and small businesses. I promised myself that I would stop buying the suitcases when I realized that I was, quite literally, collecting baggage. But this one is special. I bend down to get it. The cover is black with a pebbly texture. It has a monogram engraved on a brass plate under the handle: *P. A. F.*

What's the A for?

Axel, Trevor says. Paul Axel. I have the same middle name.

Do you mind? I'd like to have it, if that's okay.

No, you should have it. You keep suitcases, don't you? He says *keep*. Like they're cockatiels, or exotic orchids.

I could give you the five. To make up for the record guy.

Don't be stupid. It's yours.

I let the briefcase rest on my palms and he touches the sides, flicks open the latch. There's a dusty, grapefruity smell, like sour paper and ink. All of my suitcases have this smell. I'm disappointed when I realize that Paul Farenbacher's case is no different. The lining has an amorphous blue stain in the corner. There are two hinged metal arms holding up the top.

Thank you, I say.

You're welcome.

Do you want anything?

He looks at me, confused. This is the first time I've really seen Trevor's eyes since he's been home. His irises have asymmetrical spots of gold embedded in the blue. The roundness of his eyes, the roundness of his face. He is so much like his father. This is Paul Farenbacher at my age, I think. Involuntarily, I think of kissing Trevor, his smooth teeth sliding against my tongue. I look away.

I mean from the bakery. Coffee, something to eat.

Oh. No, thanks.

I'll get us cookies or something. You haven't had breakfast.

Trevor lowers the lid of the briefcase and it snaps in place. I'll save this for you, he says. You take this home.

One black October day when I was twelve, the same day I woke up to a scritching sound inside my ear (a sound that suspiciously felt like an insect, though I knew that it was highly unlikely a bug could have crawled into my ear canal; I told myself that it was a drop of water trapped in there), I found out I had been dumped by Shane DeSouza. Brad Garret came up to me at recess and said: Shane's with Tammy now, so don't call him your boyfriend anymore. Tammy was a winch-faced gymnast with a spiral perm and a penchant for a certain purple, sticky lip gloss that came in a plastic pot and had an iridescent sheen; an American brand with a French name that I knew for a fact had been tested cruelly on laboratory rabbits; a lip gloss that had been passed around to all of the girls at recess the day before, everyone but me, and when I returned to class after the lunch break on that day, my lips were conspicuously dry and un-glossed. Which is exactly why, I reasoned, huddled in the back of the playground digging at the base of the chain-link fence with a stick, Shane DeSouza didn't want to be seen with me anymore. As I cried and snuffled, my sinuses filled with fluid, giving me an ache in my temples and the ugly need to suck back tears and snot. This made the scratching in my ear intensify, almost as though there really was something in there, a tiny creature who could sense my distress.

That afternoon I was late, having dragged my sneakers through the ditches along the side of the road on the long way home, keeping my head down low, looking at stones and half-rotten leaves and disintegrating litter for poetic implications that would enhance my feeling of wretchedness. When I opened the door, I could tell that Paul Farenbacher was there. The house smelled like his aftershave: caraway seeds, menthol and sawdust.

Meredith, said my mother. There you are. Come say hello to Mr. Farenbacher. He's just brought us a gift for Thanksgiving weekend. She held a square, heavy-looking bottle in her hands.

Paul Farenbacher bent over the banister to get a look at me. Hallo, he said.

After he left, my mother showed the bottle to me—it was almond-infused Polish vodka. She uncorked it, took a whiff, and made a face. It smells like cyanide, she said, and she poured the contents down the drain. She rinsed the hand-blown glass bottle, mottled with intentional imperfections, shimmering and opalescent—not unlike Tammy's lip gloss, I noted to myself—and set it on the shelf next to the glass paperweight with a swallowtail butterfly trapped inside it.

Our house was built without any kind of mud room. After an outing, before joining the rest of the household, you were required to remove your shoes at the door, hang your coat on the hook, and slipper your way up the stairs so you wouldn't leave a trace of the outdoors in the carpet fibres. There was a banister that framed the stairs at the entranceway to better facilitate the viewing of family and friends as they completed this procedure. After years of bearing the weight of these observers, the railing on the banister had loosened, and Paul Farenbacher leaned right along with it. When I looked up, he was tilting towards me at an alarming angle.

What's wrong with you? he asked me. You look puffy. He exchanged a glance with my mother. Tell me this is not trouble with a man!

Paul Farenbacher's lightly accented English sounded knowledgeable and wise to me, and his prematurely white hair and beard, trimmed with precision, so white that it dazzled against his toast-coloured skin, made him look like a wizard or a scientist, equally capable of saving me from the mysteries of the paranormal and the evils of humanity. The truth was that I felt safer with Paul Farenbacher than I did with my own father. My father—whose car insurance had increased exponentially from the number of fender-benders he caused every year; who, when helping me with my math homework, poured a liberal amount of Canadian Club into one of our sunflower-printed gas station collectible tumblers, calling it his "magic formula revealer"; who had to wear a shower cap and rubber gloves to work and came home from the Island Farms Dairy Production Plant every night smelling like sour milk—secretly embarrassed me.

I think something is eating my ear, I told Paul Farenbacher.

That night, while my mother started dinner (*Please stay for a bite, Paul. I'm making extra. Call Margaret and Trevor*) and my father watched television (*Can I get you a drink, Paul, let me pour you a cocktail*), I lay down on the loveseat and let Paul Farenbacher peer into my ear canal with a flashlight and gently press his callused index finger against the tragus of my right ear until a small black spider crawled out, along his finger, and into the palm of his hand.

Gotcha, Paul Farenbacher said.

I bring back a cardboard tray from the bakery, with a paper cup tucked in each of the slots and cookies for all of us to share. I deliver a cup to Bruce. I give Trevor a cup too, even though he said he didn't want one. He tells me his mom is in the backyard.

Margaret is smoking on the back steps behind the house. Paul's old ashtray is beside her. Red lettering on white ceramic: *York University Class of '69*. A roll of ash lies on top of a slice of masking tape with the price marked on it.

I raise my eyebrows. That'll be twenty-five cents, ma'am.

Oh, geez, she says, exhaling a fast puff. Don't tell Trevor, okay? Thank you, honey. I bend to offer her the tray and she takes her coffee cup out of it. It makes a squeaking sound as she pulls.

Meredith. She motions with her hand to a space on the step beside her. She pats the wood and says to me: Can I talk to you for a minute?

Of course.

I know this is hard for Trevor.

It's hard for everyone, I say. We all loved him.

Margaret nods. She holds the cigarette to her lips like a dart and inhales, eyes squinting. Then she drops her hand and looks at the cigarette in her fingers. She exhales.

These are Paul's, she says. I don't even smoke.

I ask, Can I have a drag?

She passes it to me with a sneaky look, and I put it to my lips just to have a taste.

I never thought I'd see this, she says. You're the healthiest person I know.

Don't tell my clients, I say, and let the smoke out when I smile. I sit down beside her and slip the cigarette back into the notch in the ashtray.

Margaret slices the Scotch tape with one polished fingernail and loosens the flap of the cookie box until it pops open. Since we're making confessions, she says. She plucks out an almond crescent and considers it. She continues,

I'm assuming you knew that Paul and I had an understanding.

I look at her.

She puts the cookie in her mouth all at once. I watch her chewing and swallowing and I can imagine her jawbone, her teeth, the skull that is under her skin. I wonder at this: without skin and muscles, we would all be indistinguishable. Each one of us has a skull that looks exactly the same as all the others.

It was so hard for us at the end, she says.

I'm unclear whom she means by *us*, but I don't say anything.

I just wanted to thank you. She licks the powdery crumbs off like she's kissing each finger. He loved having you come over so often. He told me.

I take this in. Then I say: You and Bruce.

She nods. I know this must seem rushed to everyone, she says. But they don't know the whole thing. I just thank God that it was fast for Paul.

She crushes the end of the cigarette into the masking tape until the smoke stops and it becomes nothing more than a stub of paper in a tiny heap of black and white ash.

Boris, the big ginger tom from down the street, has jumped inside the box of paperbacks. His ears—two orange triangles with wispy white bristles—poke up over the brim. This improves sales. He's a popular cat. A small crowd gathers around him. I sell a copy of *Neuromancer*, a battered copy of *A Prayer for Owen Meany*, and a handful of detective novels that I don't recognize.

I ask Trevor if he's going to go back to Costa Rica.

I'm going to take some time off, he says. I might go to Europe. My grandmother is in Berlin.

What about the kitesurfing? I say.

He smiles. The wind will be here when I get back.

Well. If you need a place to stay in the meantime.

He looks at me and I see his chest move through his cotton T-shirt when he takes a breath and again I have to stop myself from touching him. I wonder if he knows the truth about his mother and Bruce. If it would matter to him if he knew.

We should have dinner or something, he says to me.

The woman in the blue trench coat comes back. She's brought someone with her: a short, suntanned man with a curly blond ponytail peeking out from under a baseball cap that says *J. Brinkman and Associates Reforestation* and a flat gold chain around his neck with links that move like a snake. They both touch the sides of the La-Z-Boy, drawing lines in the plush with their fingers as they talk about getting it into their truck.

I think we're finally going to sell the big boy, I say to Trevor, and something wavers in my solar plexus as I watch the transaction.

The woman passes Margaret a bundle of twenty-dollar bills, folded in half. Margaret shakes her hand and puts the cash in her back pocket. Bruce helps the man with the chair. They stand on either side of it and they use their legs when they lift it off the ground. It looks heavy. Like pallbearers, they stand for a moment to stabilize before they carry it out to the truck.

Excuse me, I say when I see the wind swatting the flaps of blue plush fabric against the chair legs like prayer flags, the men's fingers pressing into the sides of the chair, scraping it into the back of the flatbed truck that is already sprinkled with pink petals even though it's only been parked there for a minute. Wait! I call after them, half running across the lawn like a lachrymose widow, my throat filled with hot and itchy clots of tears, crying now, because I remember the last thing that Paul Farenbacher said to me, *Bis morgen*, which wasn't significant at the time, just a little thing he said to me before I left him for the night, tucked into that chair, *that blue chair*. Wait, I scream, and now Bruce is behind me, he's got his arms around me—my God, he's a big man, his hands are easily twice the size of my shoulders—he's got me, he's holding me in a gesture that is half restraint, half reassurance. You can't have that chair, I blubber through the window of the truck to the woman, who is already sitting in the passenger side, her tight red face concerned and frightened. That chair, I cry. That chair is not for sale.

This Is How We Grow as Humans

Two weeks before Franny and Richard announce their engagement, Franny meets Pima for a late lunch at Ogden Point. The café has a large outdoor patio on the water, where the cruise ships dock, near a funny red lighthouse covered in graffiti that sits at the very end of the concrete breakwater. Neither one of them orders anything to eat. Franny has a pot of decaffeinated tea with lemon, and Pima has a cappuccino, which she stirs with a little spoon. Franny notices how Pima moves: her thin limbs seem tight at the joints and her eyes make angular, darting movements. A pot of camomile might have been a better choice for her. Franny gave up drinking coffee two years ago. She's also given up white sugar, farmed salmon, genetically modified soy products, and non-organically-grown strawberries.

It's the first warm day of spring and Pima says she wants to feel the sun on her face. She gets up to tilt the umbrella so it doesn't cast a shadow on the table. She has a long pink scarf tied around her head. The tails blow off her back like kite streamers. The sunshine is excellent. Franny closes her eyes for a minute. The direct sunlight blazes her eyelids with orange. When she opens them again, the colour is drained out of everything. Pima is standing above her, wrestling with the umbrella pole in the centre of the table. Her profile is even more severe in monochrome.

Franny invited Pima to lunch because she knows Pima wanted to meet with her. This is an opportunity for Pima to put everything out on the table. Franny's not interested in playing games. She's here to make sure that Pima is okay. They might talk about Richard, because Franny did play a role in their breakup. But more than that, this is about their *friendship*. It's an awkward meeting. But there's something like relief in the way they're sitting in the sunshine. They both realize there's no way to make this pleasant, so they're just going to practise the art of being awkward together.

Can I get anything else for you?

The waitress is dressed in a black miniskirt, heavy boots and skinny bare legs. She has a piercing on her face: a small silver stud through the skin on her cheekbone.

No, Pima says. Thank you. She doesn't turn around when she says this. Once she's sure that she's secured the umbrella, she sits down. Franny notices the perfect shape of her ass, the way her slim thighs curve in dark denim. When she moves, it looks effortless. It's like she's floating back down to her chair rather than sitting in it.

Well, the waitress says.

I'm sorry, Franny answers. She makes eye contact so the waitress will know that they aren't trying to be difficult. We haven't even looked at our bill yet, she says.

It's just that it's the end of my shift. The waitress raises her shoulders.

Of course, Franny tells her. We'll be ready in a sec.

The girl bites her lip and turns away.

Someone else could take care of our bill, Pima says.

She just wants her tip, Franny says, staring into her teacup. She lets her focus go past the surface of the liquid, like she's looking into a well. A reflection of her forehead trembles in the tea. She didn't order anything to eat because she's too anxious. On the blackboard above the service counter the specials are written in pale yellow chalk. The soup of the day is *menestrone*. She can't stop looking at the misspelling. Her nervous stomach turns again, slow and gluey.

Pima looks down into her purse and rearranges a collection of crumpled-looking receipts and linty tissues. I hate being rushed, she says.

Franny sips her tea.

I haven't talked to Richard, Pima tells her. He asked me to stop calling.

Franny nods. That's probably good, she says. To give yourself some space for now.

Pima says, We might never be friends again.

The way she says it, Franny can't tell if Pima is talking about her or Richard. Franny has always believed that it is reasonable to expect to be friends with your lovers after you've broken up. It's starting to feel unreasonable to her now.

The waitress looks at Franny when she takes her money. When she smiles, the silver stud on her cheek jerks up a little. Thanks, she says. It's just that my ride is here and I have to get going. I'm really sorry. I didn't mean to rush you.

Franny glances at Pima, who's examining a business card she found in her purse while sorting through it. Oh, we don't feel rushed at all, Pima says, without looking up. She slips the card into her daybook and then pulls out a pack of du Mauriers and slaps them on the table. Franny hates to see Pima smoking. She's too beautiful to be a smoker.

Are you going somewhere for the long weekend? Franny asks the waitress.

We're going to Sombrio Beach.

Surfer?

No. Not really.

She doesn't seem to be in a hurry anymore now that she has their money. She looks over her shoulder. There's a blue Vanagon in the parking lot. A man with blond dreadlocks taps the steering wheel and bobs his head. A German shepherd sits in the passenger seat.

Have you ever been to Sombrio Beach? the waitress asks Franny.

Franny shakes her head.

Oh, she says. You have no idea. Just going to Sombrio can inspire you to become a more evolved person. When you're there, it's like you're not even a person anymore. You're part of the sand, you're part of the driftwood.

The waitress smiles again and lurches off in her black boots. And to think Franny was just sticking up for this girl! *A more evolved person.* What is she, fifteen years old? What does she know about the work it takes to be an evolved person? Her soles are thick wedges, making her feet look like magnets that she has to pull off the ground with each step.

Pima picks at the bleached white threads that fall from the edge of her denim shirt cuffs. The shirt is old and frayed and soft, with pearly snap buttons. She's had that shirt for years, probably long before Franny even knew her.

He convinced me to not talk to him for one year, she says.

Don't you think maybe it's a good idea?

It just means he wants to fuck you without having to think about me.

Franny doesn't say anything at first. She takes a breath. Paresh, her therapist, has been coaching her to redirect aggression and not take it on personally. In a calm voice, Franny says, Maybe it means he needs time to think things through.

Whatever, Pima says, and opens the pack of cigarettes with her teeth.

On the breakwater, a group of divers are getting ready. They wear rubbery wetsuits peeled down halfway, which makes them look like weird fruit in the sun. They lug their black equipment over the rocks. One of the divers needs help carrying his tank to the starting place where everyone is gathered. The weight of the tanks looks like they would pull the people straight down to the bottom of the sea.

I always knew when he was cheating on me, Pima says, holding an unlit cigarette. I knew every single time, and I knew it this time too.

I thought he'd told you, Franny says. When it first happened, I thought you two had broken up.

This isn't exactly true. What Richard had said was that

their passion had died a long time ago. Pima was cold and distant. She wouldn't have sex with him anymore. Something inside Pima had shut down, Richard told Franny, and their relationship felt dried-up and unhealthy. It had been like this for some time. He had leaned into Franny and placed his mouth very close to her mouth without kissing her. His breath was woodsy, like clipped branches. He said, Fran, you feed me. I have never felt this way about a woman before. I want to be with you for the rest of my life.

Pima looks at her. The angle of the sun catches the green in her hazel eyes, turning them acidic. I feel sorry for you, Franny. You know that?

Pima is entitled to her anger. She's been with Richard for the past four years, and Franny's not the first woman he slept with while they were still living together. Franny knows what they say about a person never changing. But there's a *dynamic* that is set up between two people.

Richard's cheating is something that happened between Richard and Pima. Richard lived with Pima all of those years, but now he is with Franny and he wants to get married. Franny is not Pima. As Pima turns mean in front of her, Franny holds this thought close to her chest like it's a smooth, warm stone.

Listen, Pima says. Richard does this. You should know. He will keep doing it. I feel like warning you, except that right now I can't stand you.

I think—Franny starts. This isn't easy to say, but she needs to find out if it's true. She tries again. I think you're still in love with Richard, she says.

One end of Pima's silk head scarf stirs in the wind. It strokes her shoulder blade like the tip of a cat's tail. You are walking a dangerous line, she says. I think you should take a look at what you're doing. Why do you hate yourself, Franny? Why do you hate yourself so much?

Pima has it backwards. And it's just like her to put on that self-righteous, patronizing tone now, at this vulnerable point, when they could truly get to something *real*. Classic Pima. She's the one with low self-esteem, not Franny. Why else would she stay in a relationship with a man who didn't love her? Everyone knows that loss of libido is a sign of depression. But she's not supposed to know that Pima stopped wanting sex, so Franny tries to respond with something meaningful and generous. I'm glad you're being honest with me, she says. I've always admired that about you.

Pima laughs an ugly laugh. You admire honesty, she says. And you've decided to shack up with a man who doesn't even know what that word means. It's fascinating, human nature, isn't it?

Heavy splashes from the water in front of them. They listen to the sound of bodies falling into the ocean and then the divers are all underwater and it's quiet again. They sit without talking for a few minutes.

Watching the ripples on the surface of the water, Franny says to Pima, You couldn't pay me to strap that stuff to my body.

Pima lights her cigarette with a pale pink lighter and stares at the water, blowing out smoke. You know that they piss in their wetsuits? she says. They wet themselves to keep warm.

If she had turned to Franny at that moment, if she could have looked at her with even a sliver of something gentle, Franny might have told her the truth: that being with Richard isn't exactly as she expected. That she's afraid something is wrong with her. That she's actually in love with both Pima and Richard.

Franny met Richard and Pima at the same time, a dinner party, so there were no allegiances at first. The party was on an old blue houseboat, where Steve, the editor of *Western Food and Wine*, was living at the time. Steve has that condition that makes him completely hairless. He doesn't even have eyebrows or eyelashes. He's a large man, always ducking under door frames, his biceps easily the size of Franny's neck. But without hair, Steve has this vulnerable look. Franny had just started as a copy editor when she came to the party, but Steve had promised her she'd be writing restaurant reviews by the end of the year.

Lots of people from the magazine were there. Flower boxes hung on all the houseboats along the boardwalk, packed with alyssum, heaps of purple lobelia. Franny wandered inside, looking for a corkscrew. Even though it was a calm day, the floor of the house shifted when the water moved beneath it. Steve introduced her unceremoniously on his way out to the grill, with a platter of slick raw salmon in one hand and a pair of tongs in the other: Richard and Pima, meet Franny, from the magazine.

He left, and the three of them looked at each other.

Do you know Steve from college? Franny asked them.

Richard used to date Steve's sister, Pima said. She wore pink sandals with sequined straps, polished toenails like pale shells. Franny thought she was very thin. Her collarbones were so prominent, it looked like it would hurt to give her a hug. But she moved easily in her body, and this grace made her beautiful.

Long time ago, Richard said, and scratched the back of his neck.

Pima smiled. I broke them up. But Steve doesn't hold that against me. Does he, babe?

Richard put his hand on the small of her back and she moved in close so her waist dovetailed with his hip. You need an opener for that? he asked Franny, and nodded at her bottle of wine.

Franny looked up at him. There was a smudge of something on his throat, like charcoal, or newsprint. I really do, she said.

It's in the kitchen, Richard told her, and led the way. Pima followed them, her sandals gently slapping the floor.

Steve has a corkscrew mounted on his kitchen wall, with a handle that works like you're pressing a seal onto a legal document. You hardly have to use any force. Franny has one too, but a different model. Hers sits on the kitchen counter.

Richard announced, It's not a corkscrew, it's a cork extractor!

It even has a little lever that releases the cork for you, said Pima. See?

I have one like it at home, Franny said. I love it.

Oh, of course! Pima laughed. You're a *Food and Wine* girl now.

How do you like it there? Richard asked Franny.

I'm learning a lot, she said. About the whole scene. The Island Chefs Collaborative, all of the wineries up-island. She faltered, not knowing what else she could say about copy editing. I didn't know that Steve had a sister, she added.

She's in Bangladesh now, Pima said. Working in spices.

She's not in spices, she's doing textiles, Richard corrected her.

Sor-*ry*, Pima said.

Through the open kitchen window, Franny saw a black and white cat hop out of one of the boats that was docked at the harbour. It had a tiny bell around its neck that made a soft tinkling sound when it jumped. She was utterly captivated by both Pima and Richard in that exact instant, and it was like the sound of the bell announced it to her.

Steve came into the kitchen and said, Two Newfies are sitting in a cabin in the middle of winter, drinking beer and playing twenty questions. You know this one?

Before you embarrass yourself any further, said Richard, you should know that my father is a Newfoundlander.

Even better, said Steve. So they're playing twenty questions and the one guy thinks of something, right? He thinks of moosecock.

Moosecock, Franny repeated, and started to laugh. Before the joke even started. She couldn't help it. She'd never had a refined sense of humour.

Pima poured a glass of wine, handed it to Franny, and topped up her own glass. She didn't look at Steve as he told the joke, but played with the ring of Cellophane that came off the bottle when they opened it. Franny pushed her lips together and stopped laughing long enough to open them again and take a gulp of wine.

So the guy thinks of moosecock, and he says, Okay, I've thought of something. And the other guy says, Okay, first question. Can you eat it?

The corkscrew was still splayed open with the cork stuck on it. Franny reached over and untwisted the cork and pushed the arms back together so it was closed.

So this makes the first guy think for a minute. He closes his eyes and thinks about it, and then he says, Yeah. Yeah, I guess you can eat it, if you wanted to. So the second guy gets excited. He goes, right away he goes, *Is it moosecock?*

Richard looked right at Franny when he laughed. The angle of his jaw in laughter was a direct line. It hit her in

the chest. She laughed so hard she spilled some wine on the kitchen floor. Pima found a cloth under the sink and bent down to wipe it up for her. The tip of the hairpin that held her hair back. One small blue bead nestled in a twist of dark hair.

Later that night, she found Pima in the tiny houseboat bathroom, curved in front of the mirror, her head held up close, her hands near her face. A flash of silver metal in her hand. Franny stood behind her, watching. It was a spoon.

Sorry to disturb, Franny finally said.

Pima dropped her hands and looked at her in the mirror, surprised.

I just have to ask you, Franny said. What are you doing with the spoon?

It's for curling my eyelashes, Pima told her. My mother's Chilean. She taught me how when I was little. All the girls do this in Chile. She tucked the spoon in a little black zippered purse that hung on a string across her shoulder.

I'm so glad that I met you, Franny said. I mean, you two are so great. She had polished off a fair amount of Pinot by this time, as well as some excellent Madeira that Steve had brought out for the guests who wouldn't leave.

We should have you over, Pima said. What are you doing on the fifteenth?

Franny had no idea what she was doing on the fifteenth. That's perfect, she said.

Oh, wait, said Pima. We've got a yoga workshop that weekend. Let's make it the weekend after.

Yoga workshop, Franny said, feeling the wine spin in her head. How long have you been doing yoga?

I've been practising for years. Richard just started. He still thinks it's kind of flaky. When we're lying in Shivasana, our instructor goes around to everyone in the class and whispers in our ears, *You are so healthy!*

You know, Franny said grandly, her hand wavering somewhere above her head, I'm trying to focus more on personal growth myself these days. I spend a lot of time thinking about how to be a more enlightened human being.

Me too, said Pima. Have you read *The Power of Now*?

Richard was in the doorway watching them. Franny felt instantly ridiculous and realized that she was drunk.

I haven't read that, she said. Is it like *The Tao of Pooh*? I loved that.

Pima was kind enough to smile at her. Yes, she said, he writes about some of the same principles.

I've read *The Power of Now*, Richard said.

Pima rolled her eyes. Don't listen to him, she said.

See, the thing about now, Richard said, and he held his hands parallel, showing a small space between them, it's that the now is so *thin*. There's just not much now to go around, is there? As soon as you grasp it, it's gone.

Franny nodded her head. Exactly, she said. That's it exactly.

He continued, So I've been working on the power of *then*. Now there's a concept to wrap your head around. I find it much more satisfying.

Pima walked past Franny and stood in front of Richard, who was now leaning against the doorway. She wrapped her long arms around his chest and looked up into his eyes and told him, You think you're funny, but you're really infuriating.

What? he said, holding his hands up. What did I say?

This morning, before Franny left for lunch at Ogden Point, Richard said, I feel more comfortable in your bed than I ever have with Pima. Even after four years. They were curled together, Franny in the front, one of Richard's arms loosely folded over her waist. As he spoke, she played a game with the skin on his elbow. You can pinch the skin there. It's so tough, there aren't many nerves. You can squeeze someone's elbow skin as hard as you can and they might not even feel it at all. She focused on the bit of skin she held between her fingers and he said, I loved Pima, it's true. But we were never able to look after each other. It was never like this.

Franny wanted to bite the skin to see how far she could go before he would feel it. She told him, Pima invited me to lunch today. I'm going to go meet her right now and see what she has to say. Franny thought it would be better if she said that Pima was the one who extended the invitation. It was only a twist on the truth, and he didn't need to know absolutely every detail about everything she did. Isn't a healthy relationship based on autonomy, and respect for each other's privacy?

Richard said, Franny, I have to tell you something.

Franny took a breath. Okay, tell me, she said.

I think I washed something of yours I shouldn't have.

Franny turned around to face him, rotating her hips as she twisted herself under the sheets. Did he even hear what she'd said? She put her hand on his shoulder. His grey T-shirt felt coarse against the palm of her hand. Richard never used dryer sheets. When he did the laundry, the clothes crackled with static and hard edges. What was it? she asked.

A shirt, he said. A really pretty shirt.

Let me see it, she said. Did it shrink?

He pulled out a small, puckered piece of turquoise silk from under his pillow. It had been a beautiful blouse, cut on the bias so it flared slightly at the waist. Olive green lace around the deep neckline. A friend brought it back from Milan for her birthday last year. It was the size of a napkin now.

Oh no, Franny sighed. That one.

I thought it was in the pile, he said. I just took the pile.

It's okay, she said.

Let me make it up to you. He dropped it onto the floor and pulled her into his chest. His shirt smelled hot and clean and it was rough against her skin.

You should learn to use fabric softener, she told him.

He brushed her hair away from her face and kissed her. I'm a man, he said. Men don't soften things. He sat up and straddled her in the bed. He pulled the sheet sideways over her chest so she wouldn't be cold. Good morning, he said.

I have to get ready, Franny said. I slept too long. You have to let me out of this bed.

Am I holding you here against your will? His hands raised in surrender.

She saw a dark spray of underarm hair through his open sleeve. His chest pressed tight against the fabric of his T-shirt. Pinned underneath Richard's thighs, Franny relaxed. It was just a blouse, after all.

You make me feel like a complete person, she said. It's hard to leave you.

Then don't, he said. He brought his thumb to his mouth and licked it. With a purposeful look, like he was about to rub a stain out, he slipped his thumb between her legs. He moved it slowly inside. She could tell by the way he was watching her that he knew he had her. His eyes were thick and bright.

That's it, he said. That's right. Yes. He took out his thumb and bent down and pushed his head under the sheet and began to lick her in broad strokes. She thought of Pima. She shouldn't have thought of Pima, but she couldn't help it. She thought, He has licked Pima in this very same way. He has said to Pima, That's it, yes, and he's felt her move her thin brown hips in bed against his face and mouth until her whole body started to shake and she made sounds just like she's making now. That morning, it felt like Richard had his head between her legs. It felt like a tongue and two fingers. It was like the thought of Pima could turn Richard from a lover into a man who is just licking.

The breeze becomes a gust of wind and the cold air brings goosebumps to Franny's skin, a rash of cold pinpricks. Since this morning with Richard, her skin has become hypersensitive. She can sense the slightest change in temperature and humidity from the way the hairs on top of her wrist react to a breeze. She feels the atmosphere flicker electrically within her. It is not unlike fear.

Pima watches the divers on the point. She wants something from Franny.

I dare you, Fran.

Franny looks at Pima's profile in the sun. Her pink head scarf has tightened her features like a tourniquet, the edge of her nose sharp. Shadows make little pools under her eyes. She looks tired, or ill. Another wave flips in Franny's stomach and she recognizes the feeling as something primeval, but she doesn't want to name it. Pima's hand rests on the table, the cigarette a single straight line rising out between two fingers like a smokestack.

Come on. I've always wanted to get my diver's certificate, Pima says. I dare you to do it with me.

Franny shakes her head. No, she says.

Come on.

Franny's not good in the water, and Pima knows this. Franny snorkelled once in Hawaii last year. She was there writing a piece on a raw food restaurant on the Big Island. After one lunch, she wrote in her notebook: *Luscious lasagna, tomatoes tender and cool, basil so fresh the flavour startles you.* She wrote, *Strawberry and mango pie, sweet pink, makes your tongue sensitive and hesitant, celebratory.* She wrote, *This is what it is like to swallow life.* That afternoon, she tried snorkelling. She was buzzing from all the living nutrients in her system. She rented the mask and fins from a girl with orange lipstick who worked the front desk at the hotel. It was all she could do to keep her face in the water. The fish were fluorescent, darting, frightened. Her heart shouted in her ears and throat. Each time she lifted her head, she was farther from shore and would paddle to get in closer. There were yellow striped fish and white-looking ones with long pointed noses, their whole body in line with their nose. She inhaled ocean at one point. Came back to shore spluttering, feeling transparent.

There's that thing where you can go crazy if you go too deep, Franny says.

We won't go too deep.

The bends. I think it's called the bends. I'm terrified of the water anyway.

I can get us a great deal on the gear. I know a girl. She could loan you her suit.

You aren't listening to me, Franny says. Why would you even ask me this?

This is how we grow as humans, Pima says. We face our fears.

The waitress skips out to the van. She fiddles with the door handle, tugging at it until it opens. She pushes against the German shepherd to make room for herself. Franny watches the man with the dreadlocks to see if he will kiss her. Is he in love with the waitress? Do they have a satisfying, stimulating sex life? Does she ever think of someone else when he's making love to her? The dog is in the way, wagging his tail in front of his face, so Franny can't see anything.

Pima balances the cigarette between her long fingers. She flicks her thumb, sending ashes into the air. Franny fishes out the slice of lemon from the bottom of her cup and puts it in her mouth, sucks the tea out of it.

You tell Richard, Pima begins.

The tip of her cigarette disintegrates into ash. Franny flattens the lemon pulp with her tongue and chews it, rolls bits of bitter rind around the back of her mouth.

Then Pima says, Oh, I don't know. Maybe I asked for this.

The breakwater is now empty save for a twisted black cloth, or maybe a shoe—it's hard to tell from where they're sitting. The van pulls out of the parking lot with a ripping sound, gravel under the tires.

It's late, Pima says. I have to do some things. She slides her handbag off the back of her chair and hooks it onto her shoulder, a brown lozenge of leather fastened with a pewter buckle. Good luck with Richard.

Franny tells her, We never meant to do anything that would hurt you.

Pima points a finger at her. That's so sweet, she says. You're saying *we* already.

Franny watches the way Pima moves. Her purse hovers at her side as if it's the curve of her waist that holds it in place, as though the straps are merely decorative. The way her arm hangs from her collarbone is mesmerizing. Pima's arms are suspended weightlessly from her shoulders at two perfect ninety-degree angles. She thought that Pima was moving tightly before, but now Franny marvels at such a delicate connection, the clasp of shoulder blade to collarbone fine and precise.

Wait, Franny says.

Pima stops. She turns around.

Franny stands up. She can't think of what it was she wanted to say.

You're perfect, she says.

Oh—how unfortunate for it to come out that way! She moves closer to Pima and tries again.

What I meant is, I want us to be friends.

Pima looks her up and down and says, You are a piece of work.

Franny takes Pima's hand. It's a formal gesture. Aware of how absurd she looks, but unable to stop herself, trying to do it as gracefully as she can, she presses her face into Pima's hand. She slides her face down until her lips meet Pima's fingertips. She resists the urge to put them in her mouth. They smell like cigarette smoke.

When she looks up, she sees Pima's face moving closer to her own and Franny thinks Pima is going to spit in her face. What she does is this: Pima kisses her on the mouth. It's a hot, persistent kiss and it tastes dry, her smoky breath mixed with rose-flavoured lip balm and the bitter press of coffee.

There, says Pima. You got what you wanted, didn't you?

Franny stares at her.

God, you're such a coward, says Pima.

When Franny gets home, the door is unlocked. She pushes it open but feels afraid to go inside. It feels like a plum is lodged in the base of her throat. The paint is peeling all around the door frame. Flakes of dark brown curl and crack into an archipelago she's never noticed before. She realizes that she's tense: she jumps when she hears a screen door shut behind her. It's just the neighbour, with a yellow cloth in his hand. He smiles at Franny, waving the cloth like a flag. In his driveway there's a bucket full of suds and a sponge lying in a puddle. He's been washing his bicycles. He has three of them—two mountain bikes and a racing bike with curved handles.

Are you waiting for somebody? he asks her.

I was just looking at the door frame, Franny says. I think it needs to be repainted.

It's that ocean air, he says. You gotta love it.

When she goes inside, Franny finds Richard in the kitchen peeling prawns. He rinses his hands under the faucet before hugging her. His arms make a cold-water belt around her waist, but his neck is warm when she leans into it. He smells like salt and fish.

I'm taking the tails off, he tells her. I know you like them better that way.

That's not very gourmet, she says. Not very *Food and Wine*.

I didn't know if you wanted red or white, he says.

I'll open the wine, she says. You keep doing what you're doing.

She finds a bottle of red in the cupboard next to the sink. A bowl on the counter is filled with a pile of prawns that look like jelly, the colour of bruises.

How was it? he asks.

She's angry, Franny says. She told me that you've always been unfaithful and that you'll probably cheat on me.

He peels two prawns before saying anything. Then he says, Pima can be judgmental. Did you tell her about us? I mean, getting married.

No, she says. I thought you could tell her that.

She uses the point of a paring knife to slice the black shrink wrap that's around the bottle neck and peels the rest off with her fingers. She's going to take diving lessons, Franny tells him.

Pima's been saying that for years.

I might do it with her.

Franny puts the bottle neck under the lever and pushes.
Richard scoops the prawn shells out of the sink with his hand and throws them into a plastic bag. He turns around to face her, drying his hands on his jeans.

Are you serious?

Why not? she asks him.

I thought you hated water, he says. He takes the wine bottle from her hands now that she's opened it. He pours her a glass. Then it's like he's talking to himself. He says, Never mind. I think it's great. Of course, you two are friends, you do things together. That's great.

Franny's eyes follow the dark streaks up and down his thighs from where he wiped his hands. I never said that I hated water, she says. Then, We're going to have to eat something else with the prawns. I'll make a salad.

He bows and hands her the wineglass. As you wish, he says.

Something chirps near his waist. His cellphone. He reaches for his side with one hand, as though he's wearing a holster, and pulls the silver phone out. His eyes narrow at the little screen in his hand. He recognizes the number and looks up and says, Sorry, Fran, I have to take this.

He leaves her in the kitchen. Hello, he says. The hydraulic pull of the screen door separates them. The last thing she hears him say is, It's you. Yes, yes, no, it's fine. How are you?

Franny stands in the kitchen smelling ocean from the sink. There are prawn legs that Richard has missed stuck to the edge of the sink and part of one shell, pale blue, curled in the drain. The raw prawns in the bowl look like they're melting into each other. They don't even look like they used to be alive. They could be anything.

One Thousand Wax Buddhas

I've tried to think how it started, since you keep asking. It was right after the Island Daze craft sale, the day Stu and Olivia came for dinner. The cat had diarrhea. I knew it was my fault, I knew I'd given her the wrong kind of food, which is exactly why I was so pissed when I found the soft spread hardening on the mat by the door. You know how that is—I was mad because I could have prevented it. Story of my life.

You fed her Cat Chow, Robin said. You know she's allergic to it and you gave it to her anyway. Robin's light brown eyes had that glassy look. Sticky, like maple syrup.

I'm sorry, I told her, I thought it wouldn't hurt her if I just gave it to her once. And it was all they had.

She just looked at me with holes where her pupils should be, as if to say: *Typical.*

I couldn't think of anything else to tell her, which I suppose *is* typical. I'm that guy, I know I am. I have no sense of subtlety or social delicacy. I make Robin roll her eyes and throw up her hands. Had I believed her when she told me about the allergy to chicken protein? Yes. Did I think one bag of Cat Chow was going to make the cat sick? No.

I'm sorry, I said. How can I make this better?

Robin said in a papery voice, Keane, the cat will get over it. I just hate cleaning it up.

I'll clean it, I told her. It came out angrily, which is not how I meant it.

You clean it, then, she said. I'm going to work. Her voice was thin.

Work was about a hundred feet away, in a studio out back. We made candles there. We were coming to the end of our countdown for the season—Christmas orders start in August, believe it or not—and there was only one more week before they would all be polished, packed into boxes and swaddled with plastic wrap onto wooden pallets, and shoved into a transport truck and driven west to Toronto for the first round of shows. We were going to meet them there later. We always flew with WestJet because Robin didn't trust Air Canada.

Not only is candle wax heavy—it's delicate. I wrap every single candle in four layers, like it's glass, so it won't get nicked during shipping. First I give it a close skin of tissue paper, then a sheath of bubble wrap, then a sleeve of newspaper, and only then do I slide it into a cardboard box. I put about fifteen boxes on a pallet. I seal the boxes with packing tape and wrap everything onto the pallet with stretches of plastic, and then I just cross my fingers that the guys at Manitoulin Transport don't stick their forklifts into the boxes like they did two years ago. Stabbed the wax right through the box, ruined a day's sales. Nine candles per layer times four layers equals thirty-six candles at twenty-five dollars apiece equals nine hundred dollars per box. My mind works in equations. I can't help it—I get it from my father, a produce man, who worked for Loblaws when I was growing up. Remember those William Shatner commercials? By gosh, the price is right.

Every summer, we book a craft table at the community centre for the Island Daze Celebrations. That's *Daze* spelled with a *z*. Candles aren't the only export for this island, if you catch my driftwood. There are events for everybody: a cardboard boat regatta, a craft sale, a pie-eating contest, a prize for the best salalberry jam. On the last night, a local band plays the community hall. The music is usually good. Everyone gets a chance to shake and flap around on the dance floor.

Robin worked the sale this year. I stayed home to finish our numbers for that day. It was a Thursday. We were only slightly behind on production at that point—still doing well, considering it was only early July. But we had invited Stu and Olivia for dinner on Friday, which would mean lower numbers. And we were both planning to take Saturday night off, which was Robin's birthday. I was working overtime to make up for it.

When she got home, Robin told me what happened. The postal clerk, Maryanne, was giving away balloons to the kids. The balloons were blue, green and white, the same colours as our community flag. Ocean, forest and sky.

We had piles of balloons, Robin said. We were mauled by the kids.

They were helium balloons? I asked.

Tons of them, she said. One kid asked, Can I have the last white one? Then another kid yanked it out of my hand right in front of him. It was madness. Then they started sucking it and squeaking at each other. The sound of all of those little voices around me. God.

Their parents let them inhale it? I said, with some tone in my voice.

She looked at me.

It's bad for you. They shouldn't have been inhaling it.

Come on.

No, it's bad. The parents were doing it too? It's not good for your brain.

Why is it so bad?

You inhale it, Robin. Your body absorbs it.

I don't think it's so bad. Helium is really stable. It's inert.

It kills brain cells.

Keane, helium is really difficult to split.

What is that supposed to mean?

My wife has always been too intelligent for me.

So on Friday morning I cleaned up the cat's mess like I said I would, and by the time I got to the studio, Robin was already in the back filling the Buddha moulds with blue wax. She said, Keane, I meant to tell you this, there's a strange sound in the car.

What kind of sound? I asked.

When the heater's running, there's this sound, she said. Like: *rrrrrrrrrr*.

When did you notice it?

Last night, coming back from Island Daze.

And it's a whirring sound.

No, she said. More like a rattle. I hit a pothole on Mary Point Road and then the fan started rattling. It's pretty loud.

Let me take a look, I said.

Keane, she said. Her voice thin and grainy, uncooked rice.

I tried not to get sucked in. What is it? I asked calmly.

The mileage. It's listed there. Seven seven six three oh seven.

What?

It's there, she said. Talking to herself now. *Seven seven six three oh seven.*

Look at it this way: 7/7/63/07. Do you see it? Robin sees these things. She can read the patterns. I would never see this stuff if she didn't point it out, but once you see it, you can't unsee it. She was born on July 7, 1963. She was trying to tell me that it was there in the mileage. That it was a sign. The last two numbers—07—that's this year.

I didn't ask her to explain it to me. I didn't want to get into it. But I knew the day was going to be a writeoff as far as production went. Robin was filling another set of moulds, but I meant to get a whole box of cubes finished and priced and packed before the next day. I didn't want us to work so much on her birthday, like I said before.

Before going under the hood, I checked the mileage. There it was: 00776307. A coincidence, right? I put the key in the ignition and turned on the heat and listened for myself. A loud, sick-sounding *fwap-fwap-fwap* reverberated through the dash. I turned the fan on low, and it rattled more quietly. Then I turned it off and thought about how on earth I was going to get in there, to get at the fan itself. The car needed a good vacuum. There were raisins and dried cranberries scattered on the floor mats and stuck inside the crevices of the stick shift and the cup holders. A while back, Robin had an accident with a bag of trail mix. She hadn't vacuumed since then—it had been about three weeks. I guess you tend to let things go when you're in Christmas production. I noticed that there weren't any nuts left in the mess—just the raisins and berries.

It was no easy task getting into the heater from under the hood. I fumbled and heard my father's voice come out of my own mouth, *motherfucker goddammit*, as I twisted upside down to peer into the cavern of the Honda's innards. I screwed my hand into the space I saw next to the glove compartment, thinking the fan should be right next to it. My fingers landed on something soft. I should have grabbed my headlamp.

I hitched my neck at the most uncomfortable angle I could manage and was rewarded with a better view. There was a nest. Snipped bits of plastic and chewed-up fibres from a hole in the car seat, a pile of peanuts sitting cozily on the ledge of the glovebox. And right beside it, the plastic wheel that sits in the heater. I pulled it out. The poor mouse must have been in his nest when Robin hit the bump. Knocked right out of bed and straight into the rotors. The fan tore his body to shreds. There weren't even any bones left. But his head was whole, and his eyes were still open, wide and scared to death.

The car wouldn't start after I put the fan back in. I took it out and put it back in five times before kicking the damn thing and shouting at it again. *Goddammit Jesuseffingchrist.* The car was out of commission and it was the start of our busy season.

Stu and Olivia are our closest neighbours—they live about a kilometre down the road. When they came for dinner that night, they brought their baby, Morgan, with them. It's all the rage now, apparently. Gender-neutral baby names. Morgan is a girl, but you still can't tell to look at her. She's one and a half years old, but big and tall, so she looks more like a really slow three-year-old.

It was like Hurricane Morgan hit our house. It's not her fault. We should have baby-proofed more than we did. She shredded three pages of Robin's life drawing book. Just ripped them out. In hindsight, did I know it was a bad idea to leave the book out on the coffee table? Yes. Did I jump up to save the book as soon as Morgan got her hands on it? No. Why? I was trying not to be *uptight*. I was trying to be *laid-back*. Then these cork coasters that we have on our glass coffee table—they're not important, right, they're just coasters—she tore those to pieces and threw them around the room.

Olivia and Stu watched their baby rip our things apart with polite and amused looks on their faces, like they were watching a recital. At one point, Stu did take the book out of her hands and he said, No no Morgan. Then he looked at me and shook his head as if to say, *She thinks she can read already!* before he placed the book on the top shelf where she couldn't reach it.

Robin sat quietly in the brown armchair, smiling at everyone, but she was pinching her nail beds. She was pressing so hard, the skin of her fingertips turned white. I was worried about her. It had been a stressful day—the cat was sick, there was something wrong with our car, and Robin had heard something on the CBC that had made her anxious. Also, it was the day before her birthday. Sometimes her birthday makes her tense. I know when she's nervous. She has a bad habit of biting her lips, her cuticles, the insides of her cheeks.

She stood up, left the living room, and went into the kitchen—our house is small, the kitchen is part of the living room anyway—and she opened the oven and lifted the edge of the tinfoil and told us, Dinner is ready! She was rushing it a little. But I was just about ready for the night to be over too.

Okay, said Olivia. Just let me give her a quick change before we sit down.

She took Morgan into our bedroom. Robin stood at the kitchen sink, looking out the window. Stu asked me about work. I told him, The countdown is on. You know how it gets.

Stu nodded. Tell me about it, he said. We're so behind. It's impossible to work at the same pace now, with Morgan. We even had to cancel our table at Island Daze this year. We didn't have time.

Robin had to do the Daze on her own yesterday, I said. I had to work too.

Stu and Olivia are jewellers. They make wispy little earrings and fragile-looking necklaces with microscopic glass beads and silver wire. They use a magnifying glass and tweezers to build each piece. The wire is thin and light, like two-pound test.

Olivia came back into the room with Morgan, handed her to Stu, and took the white bundle of cotton diaper into the kitchen. Robin used our two blue pot holders to lift the dish out of the oven. She'd made shepherd's pie—vegetarian, for Stu and Olivia—with wild mushrooms and lentils and tarragon bubbling underneath mashed potatoes. Olivia found our compost container on the counter. She opened the lid, unwrapped the diaper, and dumped the contents into the pail. Then she refolded the diaper and tucked it into a plastic bag. There was a bad smell. It permeated the kitchen and reached us in the living room before you could say, *Holy crap*.

It was a perversely poetic ending to an altogether shitty day.

Robin and I almost had a baby. We lost her. We were young. Many of our friends were having children and I wanted us to have one at the same time so that the kids could grow up together. Robin was nervous. She couldn't see herself as a mother. But I knew I wanted to have a child with her, and after months of talking about it, she changed her mind. After four months of a hardening belly, Robin started to bleed. I drove her to the doctor, who said she should go to the hospital. It was a stormy night, which meant a rough ride on the car ferry. The boat moved over the waves in long, sick humps, up and down. On the way down, it looked like we were headed to the bottom of the sea. Sea water sloshed over the windshield. I found myself reaching over Robin's seat to be her second seat belt, as though my arm could save her from sinking. At the hospital, they told us that the baby had died. She had died weeks before, but Robin's body had held on, hadn't allowed a miscarriage.

Everyone expected that we'd want to try again. But Robin said no, and I understood. And, you know, the world just went on. Our friends' kids grew up and we all kept making up our lives the way we always did. We turned out okay.

This happened a long time ago. September 18, 1987. I think about what our life would have been like. We named her Julie. She would be twenty years old now. That's exactly how old Robin was when we got married.

See, the way time circles?

We stopped using paraffin about two years ago. Robin said that I'd been breathing too much of it, that it had started to affect my brain. She was probably right. I have short-term memory loss. It's pretty bad. I can ask you the same question three, four times in a row. This could also be because I'm getting old, but Robin said no, it's the fumes. So we started to use this new wax—EcoSoya, a 100-percent all-vegetable wax made from soybeans. It's remarkably stable, even when you re-melt and reuse it. We had it shipped from the Gelluminations Project out of Kansas. Don't get me started on candle gels. I think they're wrong. It just so happens that this place also handled the soy wax that we needed.

We had an article in *InStyle* magazine last year. Well, a picture, and our website address underneath: *www.keanecandles.com*. We got a lot of response from that one picture. It was only about two inches by two inches, one of the sunburst carvings—but the orders nearly killed us. A glossy American magazine, it's the golden egg for us up here. We also sold our candles to a few famous people. Drew Barrymore, for one. Gillian Anderson. Mae Moore. You've never heard of Mae Moore? She's a lovely woman. And that guy who wrote that detective novel about the artist. It was big last year, you know the guy. I can't pronounce his name. No—not Oprah. She didn't hear about us in time, I guess.

Are you a cat person or a dog person? I've always loved dogs. I grew up with a black Lab. But we travel too much for a dog. We got the cat when she was still a kitten. She was probably too little to be separated from the litter. Her tail stuck up like a toothpick. Maggie. She's black and white. When she eats kibble, it sounds like knuckles cracking.

This is what happened five years ago. I came back to the island after a weekend away. I had been on the mainland picking up flats of beeswax from Queen Bee Wholesale. The car smelled like sweet honey. It was a good drive home. No traffic on the bridge. I was the last car on the early ferry, which meant I got home an hour before I thought I would. It was Robin's birthday. I had a salmon in the back of the car and I wanted to smoke it on the grill with arbutus leaves.

I knew something wasn't right as soon as I pulled into our drive. The front door was wide open.

At first, I thought someone had broken into our place and destroyed everything inside it. I couldn't get in the house because of the rubble. Then I saw that it was something else: Robin had arranged shards of broken glass and pottery in a straight line from the front door right along the hallway. Then the line curled into a spiral that filled the entire living room. The shards were arranged by colour. She'd broken everything that could have been broken. Our plates and bowls, our glasses, the mirrors and picture frames. The Japanese glass fishing float. The face of the clock. The Tiffany rip-off lampshade. The Pyrex cooking dishes. She'd constructed a massive sculpture from the shards of everything we'd ever collected in our life together. It moved from translucent blues and greens to opaque colours that shifted into a rainbow, with white in the centre of the spiral. It covered most of our house. I didn't know we owned so much that could be broken.

She was happy to see me. She wasn't upset. Her eyes were unfocused because she'd been concentrating so hard. For how long? Two days, she told me.

She stood up. Her ankles were cut. Her fingers smeary with blood.

Babe, I said. You're hurt.

No, she told me. Just scratches. Look!

I looked.

Aren't you going to say anything?

Everything's broken, I said.

She eyed me with laser precision. You aren't looking, she said. It's *Spiral Jetty*.

The thing is, Robin runs so close to the line. She's more brilliant than most people, and so it's a challenge for her. It's hard enough to be reasonable in this world. Why do you think people live on these little islands? To get away from the insanity of the city. When you're creative like Robin, it's even harder. The same rules just don't apply. Robin sees things differently. It's her gift.

Eventually, I saw that she was right. It was more than a mess. It was beautiful. Sure, I was frightened when I saw it at first, but that was only because I was attached to all of the things when they were in their unbroken form. When I was able to see what she'd done, when she showed me how to look, I could see it: all the broken things were just things. She'd created something else. It was like one of her signs. It pointed to something much bigger, something far beyond *things*.

She's definitely smarter than I am. You want an example? This spring I was in the studio writing an email to Eli, a colleague in New York. He carves wood—really beautiful work. He traded me at the Seattle show in 1991: a few candles for a walking stick that I still have at the front of the house. It looks like there are elves and faces and worlds in that stick. I was emailing him to see if he was going to be at the Toronto show this year. I wanted the email to sound upbeat.

Robin, I asked. How do you spell *uh-huh*?

She laughed and laughed at me.

Finally, I got it out of her. She called out from the wick station in the back: U-H hyphen H-U-H. I typed it as she called it, and on the screen, it looked just like it sounded. I felt remarkably stupid.

Our sex life is really none of your business.

After Stu and Olivia left, Robin wanted to go out to check on her candle moulds. You have to pierce the wax with an awl after the first pouring, to break the bubbles that form. Then the second pouring fills them entirely, and they'll burn properly. I stayed in and cleaned up—swept up the broken bits of our cork coasters, taped Robin's book back together, dumped the compost, washed the dishes.

Robin came in after a while and told me that the lights had to be out at 10:00. She said *one thousand*. I didn't think much about it at the time. No, that's the truth. Robin's eccentric. And we turned the lights out before ten, so it was okay.

Robin fell asleep like she'd been hit with something. I lay beside her and watched her sleep. Oh, my Robin. When she sleeps, her body twitches like it's shot through with electrical currents. Even when it's resting, her body won't rest. She wore her green nightshirt with the ripped-open seam that exposed her shoulder, a sweet bend of skin like a section of an orange. I watched it rise with her breath and fall with her breath. There was nobody I loved more than this. It was as though there was nobody else on earth I had ever loved. I rested a hand on her warm hip. She moved her arm in her sleep, pinwheeled it up and around, scooping away her long hair so I could nestle my face in her shoulder. She did this in her sleep. Her black hair in a fan above her pillow, the length of it falling over the edge of the bed. The nape of her neck exposed to my breath. Our bodies have slept like this for the past twenty-six years. Our bodies found each other so easily in sleep.

When I first met Robin, I was afraid to talk to her. True story. Eventually I got the balls to do it. It was at a smoky party, an event at the York campus, north of everything. Artists everywhere. I don't remember what I said. I don't want to remember. She had interests, you know? Was she dating anyone at the time? Oh, yes. Did I think that one day I'd be saying, This is my wife? Not for a second. Of all the men who wanted her attention—and there were a lot of them, believe me: philosophers, artists, musicians, architects, a *veterinarian* for God's sake—Robin chose to marry me. Why me? I will die without really knowing. She said it was because I was good with my hands, but how could that be enough for someone like her? I never even finished my degree. But Robin. Her mind works on ten channels at once. And she's graceful. Lord, she's beautiful. She's taller than I am, and in all of these years, her skin hasn't lined at all. Except for the quotation marks between her eyebrows, which I wouldn't even have noticed if she didn't point them out to me. Right now, her face—it's—you can't see how beautiful she is.

They've told me that she's going to be fine.

We always listened to the CBC while we worked. That Friday, there was a story on the news about the gas prices. I didn't catch most of it, because I came back into the studio late, after trying to fix the car.

Keane, Robin said as soon as I came in. They are saying that the gas prices are going up—they're already at one oh two.

The car isn't running anymore, I said.

One oh two.

I tried not to get hooked by the wrench in her voice.

That was the temperature you had, the fever that summer—

What fever? I asked.

—and that was in July 1997. Now it's July 2007. It's exactly ten years later.

I didn't ask her: What do you think is supposed to happen ten years later?

She had bitten the inside of her cheeks until they'd bled.

So you see why I can't believe her all the time? It isn't my fault. I'm sorry about the cat. What kind of a cat has food sensitivities? It seemed like she was perfectly fine. Maggie, I mean.

The people who really piss me off at candle shows: the ones who come up to my booth and say in breathy voices, Oh, yes, I love your work. I bought one of your candles three (or five, or ten) years ago and I love it. I ask them, So? Do you like how it burns? And they say to me, I would never burn it! I keep it in the china cabinet, or on the dresser.

It's insulting.

I spend a lot of time making sure these will burn properly. One of the reasons I work with wax is because it's a *consumable product*. Do chocolate makers have this problem? People are so afraid. They hoard their things. Don't they know that it's all going to be gone one day anyway? None of this is going to last.

Is your mother still alive? Yes? Good. Pay attention to her while you still have her. Listen to me. When my mother died, it felt as though I'd shrunken inside my own skin. I sat for hours on the couch feeling like I was crouching down in the folds of my own body. *Mum is gone*, *Mum's dead*, I'd repeat to myself in my head, as though I would recover from the sadness if only I could become well acquainted with the information. I felt like I was little again, stripped naked and curled up in the shell of an old man I didn't recognize. It was not like this when my father died. I grieved for my dad, but losing my mum turned me into a baby. We are never old enough to lose our mothers.

One day, when she thought enough time had passed, Robin sat next to me on the couch, put her arm around me, and said, Welcome to the no-mo-mama club, Keane. She said it tenderly. She rubbed my back.

I have a theory about Robin. Maybe she lost her mother

when she was still too young to know that when we lose the people we love, we brush against our own death too. She was only thirteen. When you're faced with big grief like that, it's like a two-hundred-year-old cedar tree is falling towards you, creaking and smashing through the forest on the way down. You look up, you see the trunk coming down, and you know it's one of the most frightening things you're going to see in your lifetime. Grief is like that. Maybe, when Robin was little, and she looked up and saw that tree falling, she didn't know to be afraid. Maybe she saw something new coming, something new about life, and she moved right into its path without knowing that the weight of what was coming down would crush something inside her forever unless she got out of the way. She was only thirteen when it happened to her. I know, I said that already.

The accident happened on Robin's thirty-ninth birthday. Thirty-nine: that's thirteen times three. She didn't tell me this. I worked it out on my own.

I called her. I dialed the number the nurse gave me.

Oh, Keane, she said on the phone. I'm at the hospital.

I know you are, babe, I said. I took you there.

I couldn't help but notice: the last four digits of the number were 1976. The year Robin's mother died. Wicked coincidence, right? I'm sure it didn't slip past her.

Our bestselling product came from the Candle Escentuals catalogue: Plastic Candle Mould Item #2383987—

Buddha. The mould was just two sides of plastic, one with a bulging belly and one with a bulging butt. You ran a wick through the centre, taped the sides together to seal it, slid the bottom into a stand to secure it, and poured the wax in. Left it overnight to cool, and then popped it apart. The edges had to be filed and then smoothed with a blowtorch, but there he was, almost perfect every time, smiling at you. We had ten of these moulds, and we tried to make ten Buddhas every day, five days a week, all spring, summer and fall, preparing for the Christmas rush. We sold at least a thousand Buddhas every November. All of our other candles were hand-carved. Robin did the pouring and all of the administrative work. I did the carving: I did faces, I did abstract, I did shapes like sunbursts and stars. They were pretty things. But they were labour-intensive, especially with the new soy wax, which was crumbly compared to paraffin. Was it worth it to make that switch after all? Beats me. One carved star candle cost twice as much to make as a poured Buddha.

We were married on February 3, 1983. We lost Julie on September 18, 1987. Candle Escentuals catalogue: Plastic Candle Mould Item # 2383987—Buddha. I want to tell Robin: I can read the signs now too.

We had a brief and uncommon heat wave earlier this summer, and the humidity made me cranky. I was packing a box of cubes and the tape was sticking to itself and I lost my temper and threw the tape gun at the box so hard that it dented one of the candles inside. After I calmed down, replaced the damaged candle with a new one, and taped the box up smoothly, I said to Robin, I hope Manitoulin Transport won't fuck up our boxes with their forklift this year.

She said, You mean, you're afraid we're going to lose our candles again.

I said, No, I just hope that they're bloody careful with our candles this time.

She looked at me and said, But Keane, hope and fear are the same thing.

Now I think I see what she's getting at, but what? If we stop hoping for anything, aren't we just giving up on life? What's the point?

We talk about this stuff when she's in a good mood. Like I said before, she can be very philosophical when she's feeling calm. That day, when I was packing, she asked me to remind her the next time she was feeling anxious that the feeling will pass. She said that the reminder might snap her out of it. She said, Please tell me that it's okay to feel whatever it is, when I'm feeling it. No matter how uncomfortable the feeling. I said, Even if you start hearing messages from the television? She didn't answer that. It was a mean thing for me to say. I said it in a nasty way. To make up for it, I said, Okay. I'll remind you.

I wish I'd just asked her about the mileage. I could have just said it: What do the numbers mean? Why is ten o'clock important? I could have asked her. She would have let me in. But I was too afraid.

Did I tell you that we lost the whole studio? Everything. All of the equipment, the computers, the stock. I'm still going back and forth with the insurance company, but it doesn't look promising. They don't think they can call it an accident. I know what it must look like to them. How would *you* explain what happened?

Okay, I lied when I told you I lost everything. I have some moulds left. They're salvageable. And you know what else survived? A crappy Crock-Pot we used to melt small batches of colour in, for dipping. But to be honest, I don't think I have it in me anymore. Maybe this is a bona fide sign. Maybe I should just start growing tomatoes or something. Oh, I know I'll probably end up making something and selling it again. Who would ever hire a crusty old guy like me? People like to see their craftsmen shaggy. It's part of the mystique. How could I ever work for someone else again? I'd have to shave, buy new clothes.

I don't care much for religion. I was raised Anglican, but I haven't set foot in a church since I was a kid. I think it's amusing that everyone buys Buddha candles for Christmas. What do Christians like about Buddha so much, anyway? Is it because he's fat and jolly, like the other familiar face of the season? But it's so good for retail, this fusion of shopping and Jesus. It's what Robin and I lived on, of course. So we didn't let our cynicism harden up too much. And we got presents too: every year, we stole some of the cash sales from our own till—made it tax-free—and spent it on a January holiday in Hawaii or Mexico. Forgive us.

Robin's not like me. I would say she's more spiritual than I am. And she can be very philosophical about life, when she's not stressed. No, she's not a Buddhist. Well, she has some meditation books, some Dalai Lama books. She does her yoga. But that's kind of like stretching, isn't it? It's not a religion. Oh, I don't know. There's probably something to it. It's hard to argue with all of that serenity.

Here's a good story. You know Björk, that freaky Icelandic musician? Well, she was asked to play at a Free Tibet benefit concert. She refused to play. Do you know why? Because she said she didn't agree with Buddhism. She said all of that dogmatic denial of pleasure and forced simplicity drove her crazy and that she wanted nothing to do with it. She wants to live life large, with lots and lots of pleasure, and she's proud of that. If that woman ever starts a church of her own, let me know.

When I married Robin, I knew she had a nervous stomach, a tendency for insomnia. And she always watched for numbers and signs. Did I think it was strange? Of course. Was I ever frightened? Of course not. She was the most deliberate thinker I'd ever met. She noticed things that nobody else would notice. We moved into our first apartment together on May 5. It was on 5 Almer Road. She said, Five five five five. When I asked, she said, May is the fifth month, it's May fifth, Almer has five letters, we're at five five on five five.

I gave her a high-five.

I never thought I'd be able to see the world the way she did.

There have been many drugs. Robin has tried antidepressants and antipsychotics and all of today's new Valiums. There was a nurse at the ward after the *Spiral Jetty* day who told me that a half dose of Xanax seemed to help her very much. I didn't know what Xanax was, but it sounded strong and modern and I thought of Robin with bandages on her ankles from the broken glass and I said, Okay.

Xanax, it turns out, is an anti-anxiety pill that, paradoxically, sometimes causes insomnia. On Xanax, she said that her thoughts felt calmer, but she stayed up all night, watching the walls like they could tell her what she was supposed to do next. The doctors took her off some of the other drugs because she reacted poorly. Citalopram made her ramped-up and angry. She'd slam doors and snap at her therapists. Something else—the yellow and black capsules—made her move like a zombie. Rocking like a patient with Parkinson's disease. She was moving through oatmeal. I couldn't breathe when I saw her like that. I made her stop taking those too.

Yes, I made her stop. I'm not trying to control her, I'm trying to take care of her. She wasn't living anymore. She couldn't sleep on the Xanax. Sleep is the one thing I know she needs for sure. Now you probably think that I'm part of the problem. Listen, I spoke to her every day on the telephone when she was there. Every day. Once I asked her, what were her group therapy meetings like? Were they helpful at all? She told me, Well, a woman played a song by Tori Amos. Then she asked us how it made us feel. When it was my turn, I told her it made me feel sad. She said, Why? And I told her because it was a sad song, and because Tori Amos has a sad voice. So, that was one day of music therapy.

Look, if I thought the drugs were helping her, I wouldn't have stopped them. And I wanted to believe that the therapy in the hospital would be enlightening for her in some way, that she'd get to the bottom of something when she was there. But Robin just spent four weeks in a psychiatric ward with a bunch of crazy people. That's all. Until she figured out on her own how to make her fear go away. That's how she's done it every time. You're obviously not going to agree with me when I say this, but I think the problem is, she's more intelligent than her doctors.

I told you before that we turned the lights out at exactly ten o'clock, right? Well, that night we left the bedroom window wide open because the air was nice and warm. In the morning, I woke up chilled and feeling damp. There was a thick layer of fog outside sitting like a mattress on top of the ground. Robin was still asleep beside me. She must have found an extra blanket during the night—she was rolled up in fleece under the duvet. I got out of bed, slipped on a jacket and my work shoes, and was on my way out to the studio to get the wax melting and get things started for the day when I was stopped at the front door. There, on the welcome mat outside, I found three dainty squirrel parts: the snout, a paw, and the heart. They were arranged elegantly, in a straight line.

Maggie left you a birthday present, I called to Robin.

She slipped out of bed and found me at the front door. She was in that green shirt and sleeping socks. I got a strange feeling as I watched her. Like a glass door slid shut between us. I watched what she did next like I was watching television. Robin bent down and picked up each of the pieces. She cradled these bloody squirrel bits in the palm of her hand and started to cry.

I should do something, I thought. I should step in there, I should take that nasty shit out of her hands, calm her down, do something. But I didn't. I just watched her cry and cup the pieces of dismembered squirrel in her hand and I watched her rock, shifting her weight from foot to foot. She was so upset. I am a horrible husband. I couldn't feel anything.

You know this uncomfortable feeling you're having right now? I said to her.

She cried and shifted her weight from foot to foot.

It will pass, I told her.

They say they have to monitor the skin graft. It was taken from her thigh. Apparently sometimes the graft doesn't take. They might have to do it again. Her lungs are okay.

That's really good. That's lucky. Maybe because of all of that clean soy wax smoke. It's remarkably stable. Ha ha.

I don't know what I'm going to do.

The clouds didn't lift all day and the dusk felt like it came early that evening. Robin couldn't stop worrying about Maggie. We live close to the main road, but behind us was a forest. I told Robin that she would have gone into the forest, not along the road. I just wanted it to be a good day. I kept saying, I'm sure she's fine, she's hunting and exploring. She's a cat.

She never goes, Robin hissed. She wasn't hissing at me, she wasn't even looking at me, her eyes wouldn't rest on anything. She looked back and forth along the ground in the backyard as though there were a patch of lichen-covered rock that she'd missed.

The way Robin's eyes were moving. Like she was reading very fine print, back and forth across an invisible page. Her eyes were hectic and charged with static.

Babe, I told her. Let's go finish work. I'm going to make us something special for your birthday dinner. Just try to relax. Maggie was just here last night. She caught that squirrel.

She looked up at me, but I don't think she saw me. Her pupils skittered across my face.

We were leaving for Toronto in less than a month. I needed Robin to work as hard as I was working, so we would meet our production deadlines. But she was messy when she was distracted. She hadn't sealed the moulds tightly the day before, and the pale turquoise Buddha wax had leaked all over the pouring table. We had to scrap all ten of them. When I saw the spill, I thought, Ten moulds spilled equals two hundred and fifty dollars lost. It's something my father would have said. I felt like I was turning into my father. I felt like an asshole.

We tried to work for another hour. I dismantled all of the ruined turquoise Buddhas and dropped the wax in a pot to re-melt it, knowing I'd have to go into it later to pick out all the wicks with a fork. I counted up our Buddha stock. Then I left her in the studio and told her, Come in the house in twenty minutes. I'm grilling you halibut. Happy Haliburthday!

She said, How many are there?

Just two pieces, I told her. She didn't answer me.

I made it quickly on the grill, with lemon and garlic and a drizzle of oil. I covered the patio table with a blue cloth and cut a few stalks of foxglove, put them in a mug on the table. I struck a long wooden match and lit a thick white pillar candle. The body of a leggy mosquito-eater that had flown into the fire at the beginning of the summer was preserved in the well of cooled paraffin.

I thought, Why isn't she here yet? Why isn't she coming inside?

When I went out to the studio to see, she was in the back counting the Buddhas.

After dinner, I told Robin to take a hot bath and relax and get ready for a birthday massage. I was going out to look for Maggie. It was dark. If she was hunting, that would be the time to find her. I headed out for the woods behind the house, shaking her canister of tuna treats. *Thrumpity-thrumpity thrump.* The sound made no sense when she didn't come running for it. It just fell onto the tree roots and made the night feel empty.

Once I was deep in the woods, I switched my head-lamp off and stood for a minute until my eyes adjusted to the dark. I could see where the path was by looking at the treetops—there's a line, a clearing—and I could stay on the path easily if I kept looking up. The stars poked out at me. It was clear and quiet. I walked along the path, trying not to make any noise, and I got this feeling that everything was okay. I can't describe it any other way: just that everything that had happened up to now was good and was supposed to have happened.

I made kissing noises with my mouth, calling for Maggie, and I heard a rustle in the salal beside me. I stopped breathing. Cougar. Now, I knew it wasn't a cougar, but my body reacted. My muscles hardened, my heart pumped like someone turned the dial to ten. I felt full of rushing blood. My mind does this to me in the woods. A twig crunches and I freeze, ready for attack, even if it's nothing but a mouse or a shrew. Maybe a beetle. It happens to everyone.

Cougars have infrared vision. If a cougar wanted to hunt me, I'd feel claws at my throat before I'd hear a slip of paws in the bushes. I tensed up anyway. The body of a big cat was right there, beside me, this dark shape. I knew it was a boulder. I shook the can of tuna treats. *Thrumpity thrump.*

Then I saw her. She was on my path, standing about five feet away. My joy surprised me. She was Robin's cat—

I just pinched the ticks out of her fur, mopped up her accidents, disposed of her dead things. But there she was in front of me, and I was so stupidly happy. I lurched for her and she ran, of course, back into the salal. I caught a flash of her white fur as she ran away, a white flag waving surrender. She was running back in the direction of home.

I could smell it before I saw it. The smoke was sour and pungent. I ran after Maggie and the dark smell of scorched plastic got stronger and stronger. It stung to breathe it. Even though it was a cool night, my face started burning. I heard blood rushing in my ears, the sound of a jet engine. I ran out of the woods with cymbals crashing in my chest. And in that moment, before I really saw it, I had such an awful thought. I thought, Doesn't the studio look beautiful, all lit up with warm light?

Maggie knew what was happening. I know what you're thinking, but I'm telling you, she was there. She got to her first. Up on her hind legs pressing her paws at the studio door. What kind of cat would do that? When I opened the door, she ran inside. She got too close. Her whiskers were entirely singed off. She walks into things now. They say she'll do that until her whiskers grow back. That's how cats find their way around, did you know that? I thought it was all in the tail.

Robin's head was black and tufted. Her clothes were burning. I got her outside. I covered her with my jacket and tried to hold her, patting her down like I was drying her after a bath. She screamed at me as I did this. Her face looked strange and bare and I realized it was because her eyebrows had burned off. Her eyelashes. Her face was a smoking burn and I thought, If I can just get her body to stop smoking, she'll be okay. I didn't see any other burns. I thought, It's just her hair. There were black, wiry strands of it left on her face from where it singed up as she leaned over the flames. More ash than hair. Her cheekbones were bleeding and there were places where her skin had blackened. I need a telephone, I thought. I need to call the ambulance. The fire department.

The telephone in the studio, it's right there. I can still reach it. I turn around to see if I can reach it. The flames don't even seem that big. The fire is still confined to the back, in the wicking station. And I see them all, lined up in rows: one thousand multicoloured Buddhas, smiling at me in enlightenment, their heads burning off.

1. Consider the epigraph chosen for this collection: "All of you are perfect just as you are and you could use a little improvement." How does this quotation inform your reading of these stories? Why do you think the author put this in the book?

2. The author wrote a short story titled "This Cake Is for the Party," but she did not include it in this collection. Why do you think she chose to keep *This Cake Is for the Party* as the title for the collection? What would you say is its overall significance?

3. What complicates sex for the characters in the following stories? How do the sexual encounters in the following stories affect the way the characters understand intimacy and/or love?

- "This Is How We Grow as Humans"
- "Throwing Cotton"
- "Where Are You Coming From, Sweetheart?"
- "How Healthy Are You?"

4. Eating and preparing food is a central theme in these stories; it often holds an emotional charge in different ways for the characters. What might be the significance of the following meals?

- Mushroom lasagna in "Go-Manchura"
- Spaghetti sauce in "Standing Up for Janey"
- Sandwiches in "Watching Atlas"
- Salmon and wine in "This Is How We Grow as Humans"

5. (From Wikipedia): "In satire, vices, follies, abuses, and shortcomings are held up to ridicule, ideally with the intent of shaming individuals, and society itself, into improvement. Although satire is usually meant to be funny, its greater purpose is often constructive social criticism, using wit as a weapon." Discuss why you think this collection is or is not satire.

Discussion Questions

St. Martin's Griffin

6. a) Discuss how spirituality and religion direct the actions of the characters in these stories:
    - "One Thousand Wax Buddhas"
    - "Where Are You Coming From, Sweetheart?"
    - "Prognosis"

   b) How do these characters eventually find faith?

7. Discuss what you think motivates these characters:
   - Why does Franny kiss Pima? ("This Is How We Grow as Humans")
   - What makes Greg call child services? ("Watching Atlas)
   - Why does Carolyn want to dance? ("How Healthy Are You?")
   - Why does Magda write a letter to her mother-in-law? ("Prognosis")

8. In "Where Are You Coming From, Sweetheart?" the narrator, Christine, sees ghosts; in "How Healthy Are You?" there is a supernatural quality to the drug testing; in "Prognosis," Magda experiences an unexplained physical phenomenon. What do you think is the significance of these experiences for each character? Do you view each of these experiences as magical or real? Why?

9. Discuss the author's use of animals in the following stories:
   - "Throwing Cotton"
   - "Go-Manchura"
   - "Standing Up for Janey"
   - "One Thousand Wax Buddhas"

10. Which stories do you find more hopeful than others? Which characters do you think will find happiness sooner than others, and why?

11. Pick one or two examples of how loss can also be seen as a new beginning for a character, and discuss.

For more reading group suggestions, visit www.readinggroupgold.com.